Love Released
Book One Of Women Of Courage
Love Released Serial
By
Geri Foster

Thank You

Dear Reader,

Thank you for reading *Book One of Women of Courage, Love Released.* I know venues are filled with many authors and books and the choices are limitless. I'm flattered that you choose my book. There are additional books in this series and if you enjoyed Cora and Virgil's journey, I hope you'll read the others.

If you'd like to learn when I publish new books, please sign up for my **Newsletter** www.eepurl.com/Rr31H. Again, I appreciate your interest and I hope you'll check out my other books.

Sincerely,

Geri Foster

Visit me at:

www.facebook.com/gerifoster1

www.gerifoster.com/authorgerifoster

www.gerifoster.com

Join us for discussion of Women of Courage @

https://www.facebook.com/groups/689411244511805/

Love Released
By Geri Foster

First Edition

Copyright 2015 by Geri Foster

ISBN-13: 978-1511643672

ISBN-10: 1511643676

Cover Graphics
Kim Killion
Lilburn Smith

Author contact information: geri.foster@att.net

GERI FOSTER

ACKNOWLEDGEMENTS

This book dedicated to my husband, Laurence Foster. After all these years you're still my one and only love. Thank you for your support, and for believing in me when I had doubts. You've shown me that dreams really do come true and love isn't just in romance novels.
Always,
Geri Foster

CHAPTER ONE

Jefferson City, Missouri – 1947

Cora Williams focused on her work-hardened hands clasped in front of her and the cinderblock wall on the other side of the room.

"Well now, it can't be time for you to leave us, is it?" Herbert Grubber, the head prison guard, hiked his belted pants over his massive girth and continued in his harassing tone. "I thought you'd be here at least another month." His bushy brows plowed together tightly then the left side of his mouth lifted in a lopsided grin. "We *sure* hate to see you go."

Cora didn't say a word or give him the satisfaction of changing the poker-faced expression she'd perfected.

Not with freedom so close.

After several more condescending words, Grubber shoved a fountain pen and the long-anticipated release papers at her with a sour expression. Swallowing hard, she scribbled her name before training her eyes back on the far wall.

Her tormenter creased her copies and slid them across the battered counter. Before she left, Grubber tossed her a sneering wink. "You have 48 hours to check in with the law." A sadistic chuckle curled his lips. "Come back and see us soon, ya hear?"

Snatching up the legal papers and her meager belongings, she turned to leave the stench and rotting hell in her wake. Only a few yards separated her from hell and the outside.

Two other guards stood behind Grubber snickering like school girls, making the flesh on her arms prickle as if insects crawled over her flesh.

As she headed toward freedom, the young guard, Jim Duffer, tipped his hat politely and pushed the gate wide. "Run, Miss Cora. Get out of here and don't ever come back." His soft words were as much a warning as a plea.

Not all the guards in the Missouri State Penitentiary for Women were monsters, but those who were, could be terrorizing and malicious.

The gray overcast sky and the pending gloom on the horizon sized up the situation perfectly. Clutching a brown paper bag containing her meager belongings, she took a deep breath of free air and prepared for what waited on the other side. From behind, the iron gates clanged shut and Cora instinctively jumped.

If the good Lord answered prayers, she'd never hear that sound again. Glancing over her shoulder at the damp, foreboding walls that had surrounded her for five bleak years, Cora shivered. Today she felt she'd been confined behind bars for a hundred years and aged every day.

Across the separating crooked and pockmarked road, her father's shiny new car waited with the motor running. Her heart fluttered in her chest at the thought that he knew she'd been released today and he'd come to fetch her home.

It wouldn't have surprised her if her father hadn't bothered, considering she hadn't heard a word from either parent during her incarceration. Throughout the loneliest and most difficult years of her life, they'd deserted her without as much as a Christmas or a birthday card.

They'd turned their backs on their headstrong daughter and remained shielded behind old money and a well-respected name.

Squinting against the rain, the family driver, Franklin, open umbrella in hand, stepped over muddy puddles as he made his way toward her. The sight of his tall, familiar frame silently welcomed her back into the much longed-for civilized world.

From this distance, his smile, strained and apologetic, couldn't hide his discomfort. Age and a heavy sadness slowed his steps.

Shame, her persistent companion, laughed at her for assuming things would be different once she had been released. She was still the outcast, still the nonconformist, and forever the shame of her family. All the years of waiting lay heavily on her shoulders and she struggled to come up with even a semblance of a smile.

Sprinkled by the rain, not wearing a stitch of underwear, clothed in a plain, brown, cotton smock and wearing shoes two sizes too big, Cora stepped forward to greet an old friend.

"Mornin' Miss Cora," Franklin said. "It's mighty good to see ya."

Heart thumping, she couldn't take her eyes off the waiting car. "It's good to see you too, Franklin."

Fear gripped her stomach so tightly she didn't want the Williams' chauffeur to open the door. She didn't have the fortitude to face her father's wrath. Not with five years of bitterness and anger built up. No, she simply lacked the resilience to brave his angry words.

Being in prison had beaten the dignity right out of her, shattered any self-worth she had and left her completely and utterly humiliated. It would be impossible for her to hold up under the long overdue tongue-lashing that would be hot enough to singe her eyelashes.

After their brief reunion, she and Franklin reached the Lincoln Continental. As he took her bag and opened the door, he announced her father had decided not to accompany him to pick her up. Normally that would lift her spirits and make her feel better, but today for some reason it didn't. Instead the isolation left her feeling unworthy of his company or his scorn.

Scooting across the smooth leather seat, she inhaled the rich aroma of stale cigar smoke and the expensive interior of a car only a man worth a small fortune could afford. Rubbing her hands along the material, a chill shook her body. She hadn't touched anything this extravagant in so long she could barely call it to mind.

Franklin methodically folded the umbrella, put her sack on the passenger's seat and took his place behind the wheel. Turning his troubled black eyes to her, he removed his cap, exposing a patch of cotton-white hair.

When had he gotten so old?

He'd been with her family before her birth. Now, the years showed deeply in his familiar face. One she held great affection for.

"I'm sorry to be the one to tell you, Miss Cora," the chauffeur said. "Your daddy don't want to see you." Franklin blinked and lowered his watery eyes. "Your momma is down with a case of her nerves and he's afraid seeing you might make her worse."

Crushed by the coldness of being ignored, she averted her gaze to the side window. "I understand, Franklin. You can take me to my house."

He twisted his frame and stared her in the eyes. Propping his arm on the top of the seat, sadness pulled at the wrinkled features of his dark face. "Miss Cora, you ain't got no home no more. Your daddy sold everything you owned. Said it was needed to pay your lawyers or somethin' like that."

The air stilled and her breath caught in her chest. Pain and panic shot through her like a well-aimed bullet. Her father had taken everything she'd worked for. They'd stolen her life when she had no way to stop their injustice or greed. Sad realization prickled her skin and her heart shattered. At long last her father had lived up to his reputation as *the most ruthless son of a bitch in the state of Missouri.*

Now what?

Too stunned for words, she stared at the man she'd known all her life. Yes, she'd been the troublesome child. Always headstrong and stubborn, but she'd never warranted her father stealing from her.

The chauffeur glanced at the passenger seat. "He said I was to take you to your Aunt Rose's house, 'cause she left it to you in her will. He couldn't find no way to take that."

She hadn't heard. "Aunt Rose died?" Sadness pulled at her heart.

"Yes, Ma'am. Two years ago. She left you her house and everything in it. Which ain't much. But it's yours."

Anguish mounted inside her chest, swelling like an over-inflated balloon. "Aunt Rose lived in Gibbs City. That's several hours away."

She'd hoped to stay with her parents until she had an opportunity to apply for an appeal to get her medical license back. Then she'd continue on with her life. But now her father had snatched that from her grasp as well.

There will be no help coming from my family.

"I know it's a drive, but it is what it is."

Disappointment clogged her throat and threatened to cut off her airway. Determined not to cry in front of Franklin for fear it would only make him feel worse, she batted away scalding tears burning the backs of her eyes.

Squaring her shoulders, she put on what she hoped Franklin might take as a brave face. "That'll be fine, but I hate to see you drive so far."

"Me and Naomi are spending the night with my cousin in Joplin. We'll drive back to St. Louis tomorrow."

Twisting her hands in her lap, Cora chewed her bottom lip as dread lay across her shoulders heavy as a railroad tie. "That's fine." What choice did she have? No contacts with the outside world and nowhere to go. She was totally alone.

Having not seen her Aunt in seven years, Cora didn't know what to expect. She'd been a school teacher for the small town of Gibbs City, Missouri practically all her life. She'd never married and had no children, which made Cora wonder why she left anything to her when she had two sisters still alive and Cora's father was her brother.

After five years of incarceration, Cora wasn't about to look a gift horse in the mouth. At least there'd be a roof over her head. That may not be much, but she'd been stripped of every comfort she'd ever known while locked up. A house, no matter the condition, came as a blessing.

A strong sense of gratitude for her Aunt Rose's generosity swelled inside her chest. While in prison she'd spent years without enough to eat, no heat in the winter and she'd receive a beating if she so much as looked at one of the guards the wrong way.

Dread drew her eyes over her shoulder for one last look at the forbidding prison with its tall walls and iron gates. God help those trapped inside, for their lives could end without a moment's notice and no one would say a word. That was the first lesson you were taught.

Franklin squared his body behind the steering wheel, put the clutch in and shifted gears. The car lunged forward. "Naomi is waiting for us in Gibbs City. I dropped her off yesterday. She has Jack with her. He's to stay with you now."

"I'm to care for Eleanor's child?"

Why hadn't his father taken him?

The chauffeur blew out a tired breath. He had to be close to sixty-five years old by now. He and his wife, Naomi, worked for her parents as driver and housemaid for what had to be forty years. They were good people who lived in a world where the color of your skin could get you killed.

"Your momma says she can't stand being around the boy cause it makes her all melancholy." Franklin's disapproving tone confirmed Cora's appalling opinion of those responsible for the child. "He reminds her of Eleanor and that brings on her spells."

"But aren't they used to him by now?" Cora leaned forward. "It's been five years."

Franklin shook his head and raised his hand. "No, he and a nanny lived on the third floor of the house and they only allowed Jack to come down on Christmas morning. Rest of the time he stayed with Miss Richards. She's not a kindly person, but we ain't ever seen her hurt the boy."

"Did Jack's father or the Martin's not want him?"

"No, his family won't have the child, either. They want to put your sister out of their minds. Soon after you went to jail, they dropped Jack off on your daddy's doorstep and ain't been back since."

That's unforgivable.

Jack lost his mother and even his grandparents couldn't stand the sight of him. They'd hidden him away like everything else they felt uncomfortable around. He was nothing more than a mistake they wanted stashed away for no one to see. No one to judge.

Now, they'd decided he belonged with the other misfit of the family. Well that suited her just fine. As a matter of fact, nothing made her happier.

Doubt settled in the bottom of her stomach. Could she do right by the child? If anyone deserved to be loved, Jack was the most worthy.

Every child should be wanted by his family. And one who'd been abandoned and hidden away for the last five years might need more than other children.

At that moment, her spine stiffened and she squared her shoulders. They'd make it together no matter the obstacles. How could she ever turn away her own blood, especially a child in need? She'd do everything humanly possible to see he was loved and well cared for.

She'd learned a few things while in prison. While the world could be a hard, cruel place, she'd make a home for her and Jack no matter the cost and no matter what she had to do to succeed.

"Do you know if I have any money left in the bank?"

"Your daddy took all that while you was standing trial."

No money and a child.

And, knowing her father, there'd be no financial help from her family. She and Jack would be on their own, and hopefully they'd survive until she could find work.

Not exactly the homecoming she'd expected. She looked out the side window and discovered the war hadn't changed much in Jefferson City except more men walked around wearing uniforms and the American flag waved proudly in front of almost every home and business.

While locked away, inmates heard very little about the war. Months after it ended, one of the guards said something about the U.S. beating the hell out of Hitler and the Japs. That was the extent of her knowledge besides a few things she'd learned on her own.

"Naomi fixed us some sandwiches for the trip, and a couple of pieces of her chocolate cake. Made 'em up before we drove to Gibbs City."

"That's very kind of her."

Franklin looked at her in the rearview mirror. "Stop frettin', Miss Cora. You gonna be okay cause you a strong woman."

She wiped the perspiration from her forehead. "Thank you for that, Franklin."

Little did he know the woman who entered the Missouri State Penitentiary for Women died in that harsh, dark place and the one that emerged knew only fear and agony.

Her thoughts returned to Jack and how difficult his life had been while she'd been locked away. Yes, she'd suffered, but no more than the young boy. Thank God they had each other to cling to.

CHAPTER TWO

Cora and Franklin stopped an hour outside of Jeff City and shared the small lunch Naomi had prepared. Being on the outside, even on a dreary day, without walls and barbed wire lifted her spirits and gave her hope. Looking around at the green grass and the open spaces, the invisible shackles around her heart loosened.

Naomi's cake tasted delicious and actually melted in her mouth. She hadn't had much sugar in those lost years but one bite of her favorite dessert and her taste buds were resurrected.

Soon they rolled into the small town of Gibbs City and entered the neighborhood her Aunt Rose had once called home. The house sat on the corner of North Ball and Elm Street, not far from the downtown area and close to the elementary school where Aunt Rose once worked.

"We're here, Miss Cora," Franklin said. "Naomi and her sister cleaned up the place a little, but there's still a lot left to do."

One glance at the small clapboard dwelling and Cora realized the truth of Franklin's words. The sun had blistered off most of the paint and the porch steps had caved in. The two double-hung sash windows were intact, but so grimy it'd take a bucket of soap to get them clean.

The porch stretched across the front of the house, two rotted buttresses at each end held up the roof. Black shutters bracketed the two large windows, but one had fallen off and lay propped against the railing. Large flower boxes on each end lay empty and forgotten.

From the looks of the roof, Cora wondered if the house flooded in a storm, or why the thing hadn't blown off already. With more raw wood than white paint showing, the once welcoming Cape Cod cottage looked forlorn, discarded and unloved.

Weeds grew around the junk littering the front yard. On the north side a puddle of dirty water had accumulated in a hole that needed to be filled in before someone tripped and fell.

As she stared out the window of the automobile, Naomi came to the front door. She smiled broadly, holding the hand of a young boy.

Jack.

He looked so much like Eleanor it didn't surprise her that the child upset her mother. But Cora had a completely different reaction. He reminded her of the love she and her only sibling had for each other, and she would gladly share that love with her nephew.

"Hello, Miss Cora," Naomi called out. She carefully stepped off the porch, reached out to help Jack down then turned and offered her a welcoming grin.

Something inside Cora thawed the ice in her chest and she couldn't hold back a smile if she'd tried. Naomi had raised her and Eleanor and she loved the woman more than their mother, and with good reason. The housekeeper was a kind and decent woman who'd really cared about her and Eleanor.

Holding out her arms, Cora ran into Naomi's comforting embrace. "I'm so glad to see you."

Both women wiped away tears. Naomi bent over, propping her hands on her knees and looked at Jack. "This here is your Aunt Cora. You're going to live with her now."

Eyes wide and filled with worry, Jack asked, "I'm not going back with you?"

Sadly Naomi straightened his shirt then held him by the waist. "No, honey, this is where you belong."

The young boy looked skeptically from her to the place he'd soon call home. If he felt anything like her, he probably hoped the place wouldn't cave in around them. Cora knelt in front of him and smiled. "We'll make it work, Jack. Have faith."

He had Eleanor's straight blond hair, a sprinkle of freckles over his nose that spilled onto his cheeks and his two front teeth missing. Eleanor's love and zest for life shone deeply in his dark blue eyes. Cora knew in that moment she'd love this child for as long as she lived.

He belonged to her.

Towheaded and skinny as a scarecrow, he was all arms and legs. Evidently, Naomi had slicked down his hair and parted it neatly on the side. He wore a green and white stripped tee shirt that stretched across his chest and rose to show his belly. His thin legs were clad in a pair of jeans so big they required a belt that had seen much better days. Big cuffs brushed against brown, scuffed shoes. In her best estimate, Cora guessed if the fabric stayed together, Jack would be wearing those trousers well into his teens.

Gripping his thin arms, she pulled him in close for a hug. He felt stiff and awkward, but she knew he'd soon get over his shyness and they'd somehow create a life together.

Straightening, she looked at the house and refused to shake her head in doubt. "This isn't much, but you and I don't require a lot because we have each other."

Naomi put her hand on Cora's shoulder. "It sure ain't. Yesterday Franklin put the door back on, cleaned out the rat's nests and did the best he could to get things right," the housekeeper said, shaking her head. "My cousin came over and we cleaned good as we could, but there's a lot more to do."

"I appreciate all you've done."

"I'd like to do more, but we need to get to Joplin and then back to St. Louis tomorrow. Your daddy didn't want us wasting time here helping you get settled. I told him nobody lived in this house for three years. Not since your aunt moved into the old folks home. Something had to be done to make it livable."

"I'm grateful for all you were able to do." She put her arm around her nephew's narrow shoulders. "Jack and I can finish up."

"Let's go in around the back." Looking down at the crumbling stairs, Naomi said, "I hope you can find someone to fix those."

"I'll see what I can do."

Around back, the yard looked worse than in the front. Naomi opened the screen then shoved on the door. A brand new knob graced the tattered door. "Franklin put that in first thing yesterday. You can't be alone without a door to lock."

"Thank you for your thoughtfulness. I wouldn't have considered my safety in this small town."

Her long-time friend stabbed her with a warning glare. "There's bad people everywhere."

They moved through the tiny mud room that held an old Maytag wringer washing machine that'd been purchased years ago. Shelves and canning jars took up the opposite side of the room.

Entering the kitchen, Cora stopped in surprise. The worn linoleum on the floor shined spotless. The sink and counter were clean as a new penny. Cora ran her fingertips over the smooth surface of the white porcelain kitchen table. Four ladder-backed chairs in need of painting were scooted against the wainscoting, waiting.

A worn, braided rug covered the living room floor with an overstuffed, flowered couch and matching chair the only big furniture in the room. A spindly coffee table and a few smaller tables scattered around filled the room and gave a warm comfortable feeling about the two connecting rooms.

The bedroom her aunt used stood to the left, and off the kitchen, the smaller room would be used by Jack. "This here was used for your Aunt Rose's sewing room, but we put a rollaway in here for Jack and moved the sewing machine into your bedroom." Naomi brushed the thin, light blue, chenille bedspread. "We washed the towels and sheets your Aunt Rose had packed in a chest before she left."

"I'm impressed, Naomi. It's all so wonderful."

With her brows deeply furrowed, Naomi turned to Cora with a questioning gaze. "You pulling my leg?"

Smiling, Cora shook her head. "This is a mansion compared to where I've been."

Naomi's gaze dropped to the floor. "I forgot where you was, Miss Cora. I thought you might be comparing this place to your daddy's house."

"No, this one is much better." She looked at Jack who stayed close to the back door. "Do you like our new home?"

His sad eyes widened with surprise, probably because no one had ever considered what he wanted. He nodded slowly.

She walked over and ruffled his hair. "You can call me Aunt Cora."

He almost smiled.

"Well, honey, we have to get going," Naomi said. "I got Jack some clothes more fitting for around here from a white woman I know in Carthage." Two bulging pillowcases sat on Jack's bed. "And I managed to save some of your clothes too. They are in your bedroom closet."

"Again, I don't know how to thank you."

"No need. After all you been through and the way your momma and daddy treated you, in my opinion, you deserve more. 'Sides they stole everything belonged to you."

"I think father believes he's teaching me a lesson."

"Well, that's too bad your parents is the way they are."

"I'll find a job."

Franklin stepped closer. "That might be hard. So many men came back from the war looking for work and there ain't none." With his hat in hand, he pursed his lips together and shook his head. "It's gonna be real hard for you to make it, Miss Cora. Your daddy already had me drive him to the hospital here so he could talk to the man in charge."

"I didn't know he was familiar with the people of Gibbs City."

"He wasn't until the war. Then he went out and bought up a bunch of lead and zinc mines in Picher, Quapaw, and Joplin. Made himself richer than he already was."

Robert Hamilton Williams hadn't been born with a silver spoon in his mouth but he stole the closest one he could find. He'd swindled, lied, and cheated his way to the top. A man who had everything a person could ever dream of.

Not bad for a Missouri plowboy.

He even married a Southern belle from Georgia. Pretty as a peach he used to say. That poor little piece of fruit couldn't give him the son he'd always dreamed of. Instead, she'd given birth to two girls that couldn't have been more opposite than the moon and sun.

Then Clare Jasmine Coltrane-Williams decided she didn't want to continue sharing her bed with a man obsessed with getting her with another child. She moved to a separate wing of the house. Cora father's dreams had been crushed by a polite, frail and unhappy lady of refinement.

He could make money, but not a son.

That's why them giving up Jack came as such a surprise. Cora wondered why her father hadn't groomed his only grandson to be the heir to his fortune. The son he'd never had. One look into Jack tender eyes answered that question immediately.

He didn't have the fire in his belly or the meanness in his heart to follow in the footsteps of such a tyrant. No, that took a person capable of brutal and unspeakable acts. Jack simply didn't fit the mold.

"I'll find some way to support us."

Naomi walked over and handed her a wad of money and a large envelope. "I took several of your evening gowns and sold them to some rich folks in St. Louis. I knew you'd be needing money more than fancy dresses. I didn't get much for them, but you'll have money for food until you find work."

"Thank you so much. I don't know what Jack and I would've done without your help."

Cora hugged Naomi and Franklin then she and Jack followed them out the back door and around to the front of the house. They watched as the two servants slid into her father's brand new Lincoln and headed out of town.

A sense of dread came over Cora, and she forced her body to remain calm and her breathing normal. Jack needed her to be strong and she would. Her heart filled with love, she took his hand and together they walked back into the house. The sky had cleared and a slight chill moved into the area causing her to shiver.

Pulling out one of the kitchen chairs, she sat down at the table and counted out seventy-four dollars and thirty-two cents in change. That would have to last them until her first paycheck. Next, she opened the large envelope and pulled out a stack of papers. On top were her guardianship papers for Jack. Mr. Jack Hamilton Martin was now hers according to the State of Missouri.

Her eyes scanned Daniel Martin's signature and bitterness climbed into her throat, but she glanced at Jack and fought against her hatred. Revenge had landed her in prison. She couldn't be that hot-headed again. Going back where she came from wasn't a choice she could afford to make. Besides, she refused to allow Jack to face the world alone.

The next several pages were the deed to Aunt Rose's house and all its belongings. Cora looked around at what needed to be done but still sent a silent prayer of thanks to an aunt she'd admired her whole life.

A sealed letter inside the envelope came from the Medical Association notifying her that she could no longer practice medicine in the State of Missouri.

A profound sadness grew in her chest as heavy as a boulder and she fought tears that threatened to burst like water from a broken fire hydrant. Her dream had been to become a doctor. Despite the fact that she'd had to work twice as hard to prove she was capable, as well as fight her father's disapproval with each step.

Now it was all gone.

She pulled out a notice that the taxes had been paid for the next two years in advance from her aunt's estate.

The water, lights and gas had been turned on. Naomi must have seen to that. Her gaze fell to Jack sitting with his chin propped on his fist, looking guarded.

What went through his mind?

How did it feel to be dropped off and handed over to a complete stranger? One who'd been in prison and not sure she was even fit to join the human race again.

Smiling faintly, she spread out her release papers and pressed out the creases. The rules were clearly laid out. She had to stay away from known felons, not leave the state of Missouri for one year, and within forty-eight hours of being released she had to report to local law enforcement.

Heat shot to her cheeks and down her neck. Her heart raced like a freight train and she gripped the edge of the table to steady herself. How could she go to any lawman? She was free. Hadn't she served her time? That should be the end of her dealing with the law.

What about second chances and paying ones dues? Hadn't she done all that? Knowing the authorities the way she did, nothing good could come from meeting with the sheriff. Nothing at all.

Tomorrow.

Dare she risk the consequences of not complying? Could they put her back in that terrible place? Her eyes scanned the typed papers looking for anything that might keep her from having to go to the authorities.

Nothing.

It appeared she either did as instructed or she'd somehow reneged on her discharge agreement.

Lifting the last page closer to her face, Cora saw where the release date had been changed. After all the time she'd spent locked up, she honestly had no idea when she'd be discharged. One of the guards mentioned that she'd be freed on her thirty-third birthday, September twenty-eighth. The date written on the paper said *August twenty-eighth, nineteen forty-seven.*

Strange.

Suddenly it didn't matter. One look at Jack and she knew she couldn't take the chance to not obey the terms of her release. She wouldn't risk that something might go wrong and she'd end up back where she came from. How could she leave Jack to a life of misery? In that moment she knew whatever it took, she'd keep her nephew safe and love him forever. She needed him as much as he needed her.

CHAPTER THREE

Sheriff Virgil Wade Carter opened the door to his office and nodded to the deputy. "How's it going today, John?"

After spending the day evicting Paul Anderson and family from a home they couldn't pay taxes on and helping Ralph Bryant round up ten cows that had managed to break through the flimsy fence surrounding his property, guilt and weariness weighed heavily on Virgil's shoulder.

As Virgil closed the door, John Baxter swung around and sat properly in the chair. Annoyance tightened Virgil's mouth. He didn't like that the deputy took his job so lightly. Residents of Parker County shouldn't walk into the sheriff's office and see the second man in charge with his feet propped on the desk, nose in a comic book, listening to the radio.

Didn't show professional and made John look immature and lazy.

"All quiet." John stood, rubbing his palms down the side of his tan uniform. "I just let Carl go. He was sober enough to make it home."

Virgil tossed his hat on the rack and walked toward the small office next to the jail cell. "I need to talk to him while he's sober. We can't be locking him up every other day."

John shook his head. "He's been messed up since he came back from the war." His deputy hadn't fought in the war so

Virgil didn't think John had any business talking disrespectfully about a vet.

Virgil picked up the mail and sorted the junk from important business. "Yeah, well, we all have our burdens. He has a family and responsibilities. Time he put the past where it belongs."

John rubbed the back of his neck. "Biggest problem is he can't get a job."

"That's because it's hard for a business owner to hire the town drunk." Virgil tore open an envelope from the State of Missouri. "I found him a job eight months ago. Couldn't get him to stay sober long enough to show up on time."

"Well, I don't know what you can say to him that will change his thinking." John stepped closer and glanced at the letter. "What's that?"

Before Virgil could answer, the phone on the deputy's desk rang and he answered the call. After a few seconds, John handed him the receiver. "It's for you."

"Sheriff Carter here."

Ted Young, a man from around Gibbs City, who'd moved to Jeff City for a job as a prison guard, was on the line. Word had gotten to Virgil that he'd transferred to the Missouri State Penitentiary for Women.

"I just wanted to give you a little heads up, Virgil. A gal named Cora Williams was released from here today and according to her family she's headed to Gibbs City."

That sounded strange coming from happy-go-lucky Ted Young. He sounded too concerned and even a mite troubled.

A woman?

Less than ten percent of the people locked up in prison were women. "She trouble?"

"No, no, not at all."

"What's this call about, Ted?"

"I just wanted you to know. She's not a bad person, and I know it's going to be hard for her. I was hoping you might just keep an eye out, that's all."

Virgil wrinkled his brow and hoped this wasn't about matters of the heart. He wasn't good at those situations. "She mean something to you?"

"No, just, just do me a favor and don't let anything happen to her."

The receiver went dead. Virgil looked at the phone before placing it on the cradle. He couldn't help but wonder what the hell warranted that conversation. What did Ted mean by not letting anything happen to her?

More trouble.

"Who was that?"

"Fella I know who works in St. Louis." Virgil walked over to the hot plate and poured himself a cup of coffee. Raising the mug to his lips, he thought about Ted and Cora Williams. "It looks like one of Jeff City's castoffs is moving to Parker County."

"Really?" John walked to the coffeepot. "That's all we need. More troublemakers."

"This is a woman. Cora Williams."

John stopped and stared hard, the coffeepot and cup poised. "A woman? In prison? What'd she do?"

"I don't know. But all ex-cons have forty-eight hours after release to check in."

John put down the pot. "Well, I'll be damned. If that don't beat all." John chuckled. "We might have a pistol-wielding woman on the loose." John patted him on the back. "Hope we don't have to lock her up. That could be mighty uncomfortable, if you know what I mean."

"I wonder where she's staying."

"I ain't heard of anyone new moving into town."

"Well, trouble always comes to us. We don't have to go looking for it."

John hooked his thumbs in the waist of his trousers. "Man, the town is going to be buzzing like a beehive."

"Let's be professional. Don't go flapping your jaws and getting the citizens all riled up."

Virgil went into his office and finished reading the mail. Leaning back, he stared at the big crack in the ceiling and hoped that Cora Williams wouldn't turn his county upside down.

He'd worked hard after being elected to bring law and order back into the area. The retired sheriff had turned his head too many times to suit Virgil. He couldn't tolerate injustice. That caused a few in the area to not be too fond of him, but he had a job to do and he'd do it to the best of his ability.

That's what the Marines taught him during the war.

CHAPTER FOUR

Inspecting the contents of the icebox, Cora saw there were staples but little to make a meal with. Knowing Jack would be hungry soon, she put the money in her purse, stood, then turned to him. "You have any idea where there's a store where we can buy food?"

Surprised by the question, he shook his head and held up a finger. "I only been here one day."

"I thought maybe Naomi might've taken you with her when she bought the milk and butter."

"I think that was already here."

"Her sister probably did the shopping."

"I'm only seven," Jack said, wearily. "You shouldn't expect much from me."

Cora laughed and ruffled his hair. "You're all of seven? Wow, the last time I saw you we were celebrating your second birthday."

"Who's we?"

Cora thought for a moment before the big birthday party came to her with such clarity she could almost hear Eleanor's laughter. "Your mom and dad where there."

Such a happy day, but the memory chilled her skin and had her heart pounding like a carpenter's hammer. "Your grandparents were in on the celebration too."

"I don't remember having a birthday party."

"Do you remember your mother, Eleanor?"

Sad Eleanor eyes, wallowing in sadness stared at her. "No."

"Well, she loved you very much."

"Grandfather Williams says my mom's in heaven and I won't ever see her again."

Leave it to her father to be cruel and hard-hearted, even to a child. "Well, no one knows that for sure."

"I hope she's happy."

Touched by his kindness, she stood and cradled his head to her stomach as she fought to keep from crying. "I'm sure she is." She had to change the subject or they'd both be drowning in tears. "I remember that Main Street is only about two blocks that way. Let's take a walk."

Glancing down at the tattered, prison issued smock, Cora's stomach soured and a bitter taste filled her mouth. The garb felt as rough as a burlap sack against her skin and the fabric was worn thin as gauze. Everything about the uniform made her want to recoil, hide and shove bad memories aside.

She glanced at the brown bag she'd carried out of prison that held the items she wore when delivered to the penitentiary. She couldn't stand to look at them and not remember the betrayal.

Eyes wide, Jack moved closer, looked up at her and tugged her hand. "What's wrong?"

"Wait here. I'm going to try to find something else to wear."

"I hope you have some shoes that fit." Shaking his head, he pointed to her feet. "I don't think you'll ever grow into those."

Fighting back a grin, she nibbled her bottom lip. "Probably not."

In the front bedroom, she closed the door and went to the closet. A plain, blue, cotton dress, with a fitted waist and big square pockets hung among several other dresses. Holding the dress out to inspect, she found nothing fancy or glamorous about it, but to her that was the prettiest thing she'd seen in years. Her heart lightened.

Grasping the metal hanger, she ran her coarse, chapped hand over the material before rubbing the cotton against her cheek. Sensations of sunshine, freedom and joy sang through her veins reminding her of better times.

Visions of her once gorgeous wardrobe flashed before her eyes. Not only had she been a very successful surgeon, she had a clothing allowance that matched a model's.

All the fancy dinners and parties she used to attend mocked her and sent her reeling back to the present and the harsh reality of what she had to face.

Looking in the small chest of drawers, she found several pairs of silk underwear, two brassieres and a full slip. Thank goodness, Naomi had come up with a pair of sensible shoes that fit.

Cora slumped on the bed, clasped the garments to her face and cried for the first time in years. Sobs ripped from her throat as the reality of everything came crashing into her like a wrecking ball. The smell of clean clothes as opposed to lye, the feel of softness compared to stiff and scratchy and the normalcy of being in a real house with a door that opened and closed at her will.

Most importantly, the child she'd always loved only a few feet away.

Unable to stand the ugly smock any longer, she stood, yanked it over her head and tossed it on the floor. She wanted to stomp it into the hardwood, but didn't. Instead she kicked it into the closet and reached for her dress.

Silk underwear and a slip felt heavenly against her chapped skin. What a luxury she'd taken for granted years before going to prison. Now, gratitude for Naomi's kindness and thoughtfulness surged through her body with the power a waterfall.

She glanced down at her broken and chipped fingernails and fought the urge to hide them away in the pockets of her dress. A vague memory of getting a manicure danced through her thoughts. She felt certain there'd be none of that in her future. Food, keeping a roof over their heads and paying the utility bills took top priority.

But, none of that mattered. She had Jack.

Looking up, she caught a glimpse of her face in the silver and black mirror. Her hair had grown some since her last visit to solitary, but barely enough to cover her ears. The days of long strands of golden-brown hair were long gone. And that fancy pageboy she used to wear appeared ridiculous now. Nothing prevented her from allowing her hair to grow, but she found with everything on her plate, her appearance held a low priority.

No more Max Factor make-up, Maybelline mascara or bright red lipstick. She'd pass on the expensive perfume and the whole lavish lifestyle of a very successful woman. Now, common sense ruled the day.

Dressed in decent clothes for the first time in years, she walked out of the bedroom to see Jack's anxious face. He reached up and put his hand in hers. "Have you been crying, Aunt Cora?" The concern in his eyes touched her heart. "Are you sad I'm here?"

"No, I'm so happy to have you that I want to just gobble you up. You'll never be alone again. Never."

Content with her answer, they exited the back door and walked down Elm Street toward the center of town.

"What do you think of our new home?"

"I don't know." His tiny shoulders moved up. "Are you going to bring Miss Richards to come live with us?"

"Miss Richards?"

Head down, he spoke to the ground. "My nanny."

His defeated posture and grim face let her know Jack didn't want anything to do with her. "No, it's just me and you."

His steps increased and he nodded briskly. "Good, that's the way I like it."

"You didn't care for Miss Richards?"

"I don't know."

"Surely you went out to play, had friends over and went to birthday parties."

Jack stopped and looked at her. "You said I had a birthday party when I was two."

"Yes."

"Then that's the only one I've been to."

Sadly, things were much worse than she'd imagined. Jack had been as much a prisoner as she had. Maybe God would give her the courage to change that. Not today, but sometime in the future. First, she had to look at her adoption papers and find the exact date of his birthday. She knew it was in June, but not what day. But, even if she had to sweep the streets, Jack would have a birthday party this year.

And friends.

Turning on Park Avenue, they soon came to Main Street and the heart of Gibbs City, Missouri. A drugstore sat on the corner, a filling station on the other and a diner made from an old train car across the street. A grocery store and several other places of businesses lined the street. "I guess this is where everything happens in Gibbs City."

"What's that?" Jack pointed to a marquee.

She smiled. "That's a theater where they show movie pictures. Haven't you ever been to one?"

"No, but I'd sure like to."

"We'll have to put that on our list of things to do." While she had some money, Cora knew she'd have to get a job before they could spend much on entertainment. Right now, just being able to walk down the street a free woman felt wonderful. And if the smile on Jack's face was any indication, he enjoyed the outing as well.

Near the barbershop, three men sat on a bench next to the red, white and blue pole turning slowly and talked. Across the street, two men with a board propped on their laps played checkers. As they approached the drugstore, a lady pushing a baby buggy waved hello to several people as she passed.

Cars, new and old, traveled down Main Street in both directions, while voices called back and forth. Brand new parking meters lined two blocks, charging a nickel to park for one hour.

A man tipped his hat and a lady smiled as they passed, making Cora feel more civilized by the moment. Tin signs were hung from every post. There were Coca-Cola signs, 7UP, Wrigley's Juicy Fruit gum, and a picture of a bottle of Squirt on a temperature gauge. It brought back a lot of memories.

In Martin's Grocery Store she was taken aback by the size of the place. She felt slightly nervous at the novelty of choosing items from the shelves. Her fingers trailed over the variety of canned foods and packaged items. After five years, she would be responsible for deciding what she now ate and wore.

Careful to stretch every penny, she remained frugal until they came to the candy section carefully displayed on the front wall.

Jack's eyes widened and Cora's mouth watered. "You want a piece of candy, Jack?"

"Yes, please."

She let go of his hand. "Pick out two pieces. You can have them after dinner." He shot right to the Tootsie Roll bin and put them in their basket with a wide grin.

"So, I see you're a chocolate man."

"They're my favorite."

After examining the things in the basket, they headed to the checkout counter when she saw a Big Chief tablet and a box of number two lead pencils.

School.

That had completely slipped her mind.

Her eyes quickly darted outside to trees lining the street. Their leaves were turning and would soon be a cascade of red, gold and orange but they weren't quite there yet.

Fall.

Time for school.

Jack would need to attend this year. The thought terrified her that she'd have to let him go for a whole day. Then she realized that if he didn't go to school, she'd have to have someone watch him while she worked. There would be precious little time for her to get to know him.

She knelt down and took Jack's hands. "Do you go to school this year?"

He shrugged.

"You're seven, right?"

"Miss Richards said I was doing first grade work."

"Then you'll be going to school."

His little face lit up like a beacon. "I'd like that. Maybe I could play with the other kids."

Little did he know that this town, like any other, could very well turn on them once they learned about her past. And poor Jack would suffer for her poor judgment.

She forced a smile and touched his cheek. "I'm sure you'll make lots of friends."

She placed the tablet and a pencil in her basket then moved to check out.

"Afternoon, ma'am," the young clerk said as he placed the groceries on the counter.

"Hello," she managed to reply. "Can you tell me when school starts?"

"In four days. Right after Labor Day."

That's right, today was Thursday and Labor Day would be Monday. After the holiday the kids had to report to school. She'd have to get Jack enrolled as soon as possible. Perhaps tomorrow, on Friday. Then they'd at least have a long weekend.

"Thank you. Do you know if I can enroll him at the school or is registration held somewhere else?"

"Nope, just go to the schoolhouse and Mr. Russell will take care of you."

As he wrote down each item on a lined notepad, he licked the pencil after each entry. "You new in town?"

"Yes." She struggled with the word. "I'm Rose Williams' niece, Cora." She touched Jack on the shoulder. "This is Jack, my nephew. We're living in Rose's house over on North Ball."

"That house is pretty rundown. Nobody lived in it since Miss Rose went to the Cherry Hill Nursing Home. She sure was a nice teacher." He continued his task. "Taught me and my brother. My daddy, too." He grinned exposing a bunch of teeth too big for his mouth. "He owns the store."

How long could they ride on Aunt Rose's good reputation? Able to manage a thin smile, she handed over the precious money. "Thank you."

"You want these groceries delivered? Won't be a problem."

Picking up the paper sacks, she smiled down at Jack. "I think we can make it, don't you?"

With a determined set of his jaw, he grabbed the two lighter parcels.

Cora stopped and turned back to the clerk. "Is the Sheriff's Office still in the town square?"

"Yes, ma'am. Right between the courthouse and the fire station."

"Thank you again for your help."

They exited the store and Cora felt so grateful Naomi had the foresight to sell off some of her expensive gowns. While she received nowhere close to their real value, she was grateful for the cash.

As they walked home, Cora looked around for help wanted signs in the windows of local businesses but didn't see any. Fear crawled up her back and she tightened her hold on the bags. Still she refused to allow anything to throw a wet blanket over her and Jack's first day together.

She was young, well-educated and strong. Everything would work out fine. It had to. Jack would be enrolled in school, she'd visit the sheriff and then when school started, she'd look for a job.

The sight of the sheriff's car rolling past them hiked up her heart rate and she stopped. Behind the wheel, a light-haired man with a sharp blue gaze stared intensely. Fearful, she immediately lowered her eyes and buried her face in the sack.

Sweat peppered her body and she struggled to breathe. The car slowed to a crawl and she clutched the bags tighter, praying he wouldn't stop, wouldn't question her and wouldn't embarrass her in front of the citizens walking down the main street of town.

Her mouth dried up as her nerves became hypersensitive.

When she raised her gaze, the black and white Ford with two red lights on top had driven on. He'd either turned the corner or sped up. Either way, she allowed her heart to resume to normal and carefully stepped off the curb to cross the street and headed for the safety of home.

CHAPTER FIVE

Virgil didn't recognize the woman and small boy leaving Howard Martin's carrying sacks of groceries. They had to be new to town, but they appeared familiar enough to find their way around. And from the bags, they intended to stay awhile.

Immediately his thoughts went to the call he'd received from Ted. *Could she be the woman from the Missouri State Penitentiary for Women? Nothing had been said about a boy. Did she have a husband?*

Knowing he'd find out tomorrow, Virgil drove toward Carl Riley's house in hopes he could talk some sense into a man who'd risked his life for his country but found it hard to settle back into civilian life.

Nobody ever said anything but Virgil imagined most men came back from the war with some problems. He had. You can't send a man to kill as many people as he had and not expect him to have regrets, difficulties and torments.

Even today, over a year later, the sound of exploding shells and the thunder of Panzer tanks still woke him in the middle of the night. Many times he lay in bed drenched in sweat and unable to return to sleep. The screams of fallen friends echoed in the darkness.

Virgil didn't look forward to paying Carl a visit, but it had to be done. Carl and he had fought the war and he felt the veteran deserved help and patience.

He pulled onto Freemont Street, close to Carl's small tar-papered house. Virgil shook his head at the junk strewn all over the yard and piled high on the porch. He'd be surprised if the floor didn't fall through. Disgusted, Virgil stopped the car, turned off the key and slid out from behind the steering wheel.

Carl's oldest, sixteen-year-old Archie, sat on the edge of the sidewalk in a crippled rocking chair. "Whatcha doing, Sheriff Carter?"

"Come to speak to your dad. He home?"

"Yeah, he's in the kitchen drinking coffee."

Well, that was an improvement. He hadn't started hitting the bottle yet. *Not saying he wouldn't before the sun went down.*

Virgil stepped on the porch and knocked.

Ruth, Carl's wife, answered. He could tell by the sour expression on her face she was miserable and about to surrender all hope. Worry clouded her brown eyes as she looked around him at the squad car.

Glancing away, Virgil asked, "He here?"

Without a reply, she opened the door wider and stepped aside. Obviously, she didn't care if he hauled her husband off to jail or not. Sometimes being married to a drunk could do that to a woman.

He and Ruth had been in the same grade together in school. She'd always been a shy girl with a lithe frame and curious eyes. Now, life had worn her down to a sad woman who took no pride in her appearance and little hope for the future.

Removing his hat, Virgil entered the house that didn't look much better than the yard. Sheer, dusty curtains covered the dirty windows. A cat crawled out from behind a couch unfit to sit on and the smell of burnt bacon grease hung in the air.

Carl sat at a wooden kitchen table with his five-year-old daughter on his knee. He looked up at Virgil with eyes glazed and bloodshot. "What you doing here?"

"I came to see if I could talk to you." He motioned toward the screen door. "Maybe outside?"

Virgil walked out the way he'd come in. Behind him, he heard the scraping of the chair as Carl stood. Passing Ruth, he nodded then dropped his gaze. No doubt she knew the reason for his visit.

Once out of Archie's earshot, Virgil turned and placed his hand on Carl's shoulder. He noticed the thinning hair, unshaven face and dirty, torn undershirt. The smell of liquor didn't escape his notice, either. "Carl I know it's been rough since you came home from the war. It's hard on all of us, but you can't go around getting drunk and stirring up all kinds of trouble."

Shame reddened Carl's fair skin. "I know that."

"Then stop."

Looking at him with red-rimmed eyes, Carl said, "You think I ain't tried. I ain't looked at myself a hundred times and not liked what I see? I know I'm not good for anything."

"Yes, you are. You're good for your family." He pointed to the door where Carl's wife and kids stood. "They need you."

"They're ashamed of the man I've become."

"The man you chose to become. Change that Carl, if not for your damn fool self, then do it for them."

Tears gathered in his old buddy's eyes. "I want to change, Virgil. I really do. I want to be the man I was before I left. But I can't. It's just that we did things and saw things we can't never talk about."

Virgil wrapped his hand around Carl's bicep. "I'm not a smart man. I don't claim to know all the answers. But you can't go on like this."

A harsh chuckle escaped from between Carl's chapped lips. "You make it sound so easy."

"No, I don't. It is what it is. Me and you, we can't change anything except what we feel inside."

"I feel empty."

He knew exactly how his buddy felt. For three and a half years during the war he'd been hungry, wet, cold or scared. Usually all at the same time. He'd fought in Africa, the Krauts in Europe and the Japs on Okinawa. As a Marine he'd become a killing machine.

He'd held his dying buddies, bandaged his injured men, and buried more than he wanted to remember. The names, faces and memories visited him nightly. Never leaving him alone to return to just a plain man anymore.

Virgil looked at the family huddled on the front porch. "There's nothing left inside me, either." He nodded toward the front of the house. "But try to feel something for them."

After getting into his cruiser, Virgil headed back to the station. He didn't put a lot of stake in his words to Carl because he'd said them a dozen times before. It never did any good. For a day or two Carl would straighten up, try to do the right thing, then he'd lose himself in a bottle of gin and all hell would break loose.

Virgil knew the war had been rough on all who served. The killing, dying and fear somehow branded every military man in some way or another. You couldn't run from the smell of death. You just had to face it head on and hope this time you didn't lose your mind or hurt some innocent person.

That's why Virgil hadn't bothered to get married when he came home. He didn't trust himself with a woman. Oh, one of Mable's gals on the outskirts of town once in a while was fine, but nothing he had to work on. That scared him to death. He'd rather face a hundred German soldiers with a single shot rifle to defend himself than risk loving someone.

Men came back from the war damaged so badly they couldn't be fixed. He'd seen his share of men shell-shocked and it wasn't pretty.

Something best left over there and not brought back home for families to deal with. Besides, they couldn't help a man worn out and beat up from fighting.

***

Cora came home and emptied the sacks and put away the groceries they'd bought. She decided on sandwiches for supper since Jake was hungry and she didn't have the strength to cook a decent meal. She promised tomorrow she'd make it a special day and maybe bake cookies or something sweet.

At the kitchen table she looked across at Jack and her stomach felt like she was on a ship in a storm. What if she couldn't find work, couldn't keep the flimsy roof over their heads? What would happen to this young boy if anything befell her?

That brought to mind her mandatory visit to the sheriff tomorrow. Would he be fair? What if he told her to get out of his county?

Where would they go?

Depression settled around her again. Losing her appetite, she pushed her meal aside and stared out the window. The sun had dropped into the horizon and a chill filled the house. She wondered how to work the furnace but silently vowed to figure it out later.

"You not hungry, Aunt Cora?"

She smiled at his innocent face. "No, I had a big lunch with Franklin today on the way here."

"Where have you been so long? How come I never met you before?"

From the moment they'd met, Cora knew that she'd have to explain her absence from Jack's life.

Dare she tell the truth?

No, hopefully he'd never know.

"I've been away working."

"Where?"

"In New York."

"Is that far away?"

"Very far."

He smiled. "I'm glad you're back."

"I am too."

Slowly, he looked around their small house. "Will you have to leave again?"

"I hope we're always together, Jack."

"Yeah, me too."

A knock sounded and Cora jumped. Who could be calling at this hour? Her thoughts immediately went to the sheriff. Maybe he'd decided he didn't want an ex-con in his town. Maybe he'd come to tell them to pack up and get out.

A questioning gaze filled Jack's eyes and she forced herself to smile. "It looks like we have company."

Jack stood with her and they walked to the front of the house. She clenched the sides of her dress then opened the door. On the opposite side of the screen stood an attractive woman in her middle-thirties, with brown, curly hair and eyes to match.

She stuck out her hand. "Howdy, I'm Maggie Cox." She turned to her right and pointed. "I live across the street."

Relief washed over Cora like a clean spring rain. "I'm pleased to meet you, Maggie." She shoved open the screen. "Won't you come in?"

Maggie shook her head. "No, I just came by to see if you got all settled in. Naomi said you were Rose's niece and you'd be living here."

Cora pulled Jack against her side. "This is my nephew, Jack. He's going to be staying with me."

"Oh, that's nice. I got me a boy about your age. Name is Tommy."

Jack didn't say anything because he probably didn't know what to say to a person offering him a friend. Something he'd never had before.

"I'm sure they'll get to be good playmates."

Maggie turned to go. "I just came by to let you know if you need anything give a shout out to me or my husband, Briggs. He works at the mines during the day, but he's around in the evenings."

"I really appreciate your offer, Maggie. And I look forward to us getting to know each other better."

A dog howled in the distance as Maggie slipped away in the darkness, obviously comfortable in her own neighborhood.

They went back inside and Jack looked up at her. "Do you think Tommy will really want to be my friend?"

She knelt in front of him and clutched his tiny shoulders. "Of course, I do. Why wouldn't he?"

Jack shrugged. "I don't know. I've never had a friend before."

"Well, Tommy sounds like a good name for a pal. I bet you fellas have a lot of fun in the future."

"Maybe we can go to school together?"

The excitement in his voice lightened her heart. He sounded so hopeful. Maybe this could work out for both of them. "I bet you could."

Later that night, after Jack had washed and gone to bed, Cora sat out on the front porch of her tattered little house with the hole in the front yard. The starlit sky cast a dark shadow on the town. For the first time in a very long time, she thought of tomorrow and all the possibilities.

For a moment her mistakes were behind her and the hope of tomorrow gleamed on the horizon. She smiled at the full moon and pulled the sweater closer to ward off the chill. Tomorrow she would learn how to turn on the heater and start cleaning up the yard. Tonight, dreams of the future would keep her warm.

She stood to go inside when headlights came down Elm Street to her left. She squinted into the darkness and made out the sheriff's car as it slowly passed her house.

Fear claimed her body and soul once again.

CHAPTER SIX

Cora rose before dawn and washed her face and brushed her teeth. While seeing the sheriff's black and white had frightened her, she'd served her time and had the right to walk down any street she pleased.

For now she was content with the feel of fresh water and scrubbing of her teeth. Gone was the need to watch behind her, the need to worry about the rest of the day. She was a free woman who could do as she pleased as long as she didn't break the law.

She put on a pot of coffee to perk and went in and made her bed. Another long-learned habit. You didn't make your bed in prison, you'd find the bed stripped and you'd spend the nights shivering for a week.

She glanced in at Jack still deep in slumber. Enjoying the aroma of fresh brewed coffee, she tiptoed into his room and sat on the edge of the bed to watch him lie lost in the innocence of youth.

Panic clutched her chest, but she wasn't going to worry about everything that could go wrong. For now, she was going to think about their future. Just her and Jack. That's all she needed...that and a job.

In the kitchen, she filled her cup and went outside to sit on the porch. Today she wore a plain dress of green and yellow plaid that hung loose from the shoulders, since she'd lost so much weight. There had been a matching sash at one time, but the belt wasn't among the other items.

She didn't mind. Anything beat the scratchy smocks from the prison. And the underwear was a big improvement over going without. There had been a reason for that too, but she refused to allow her mind to go there. Better she stay close to Jack in a safer place.

As she drained her cup, Jack came out wrapped in his blanket, barefooted. She smiled and pulled him onto her lap. His head rested comfortably on her chest.

The smell of sleep clung to his little body and the freshness of his newly-washed hair touched her nose. He felt so good. Perhaps the only decent thing in her life was this little boy.

"I'm hungry," he muttered. "What's for breakfast?"

"How about pancakes?"

He sat up. "You can make pancakes?"

"Yes, I can," she said with a smile. "And we bought syrup yesterday."

He jumped from her lap and ran inside before she could prevent him from kicking over her empty cup in his excitement.

She stood and stretched her back. After breakfast she planned to register him for school and then she'd pay the sheriff a visit. Might as well get that behind her and done with.

Finished with school enrollment, she tried to contain Jack's happiness at the knowledge that he'd be playing with other kids his age and he'd have his very own desk.

The teacher, Miss Ruth Potter, couldn't be out of her twenties and appeared very nice and caring. Jack took to her right away.

He skipped ahead of Cora, laughing and chattering like a happy child. A vast improvement from yesterday when he looked so scared and unsure. His happiness grew infectious as a wide smile stretched her lips.

For the first time Cora looked forward to the life she and Jack would carve out in the little town. They'd both make friends and laugh and maybe everything would be okay.

They reached the town square long before she'd built up enough courage to come face to face with the person who would have control over her life. Passing the courthouse, she stopped at the sheriff's office. Not wanting Jack to know the whole truth, she asked him to wait for her outside with a warning not to leave the area.

She opened the door and stepped to the deputy's desk. "Can I help you?"

"My name is Cora Williams and I've been instructed to report to the sheriff."

"Have a seat. I'll see if he has time to see you."

Cora didn't take the small chair offered. Instead she clutched the envelope containing her release and Jack's guardianship papers.

The deputy retuned, opened the door and a tall man with dark blond hair, lighter eyebrows and blue eyes entered the waiting room. He was tall and lean, yet muscular. He wore a khaki shirt with matching trousers. His black shoes were polished and he had a badge on his chest near his heart.

He'd been the man in the squad car.

He held out his hand. "I'm Sheriff Virgil Carter. John here tells me you're Cora Williams."

She swallowed a lump in her throat the size of an onion as the deputy eyed her cautiously. *Did he expect her to shoot someone?* "Yes, sir."

The sheriff's gaze fell to the envelope she held. "Let's go into my office."

She glanced out the window at Jack waiting patiently near the door. She followed quietly, wanting to get the ordeal over with. It surprised her when he left the door ajar, but still her insides trembled and her hands shook. The coffee she'd enjoyed this morning didn't want to stay in her stomach. The sheriff could do anything he wanted to her and she wouldn't dare utter a word.

He offered her a chair. She sat on the edge and laid the envelope on his desk. "That letter says I have to report to you."

A flash of surprise covered his face when he read the official papers. "You just get out of prison?"

She bowed her head. "Yes, sir."

As she waited, he took the envelope and pulled out the paperwork. "It says here you have legal custody of your nephew?"

"Yes, sir, his name is Jack."

"You married?"

She blinked several times, not expecting the question. "No, sir."

He rubbed his jaw. "Says here the boy is seven years old." He leaned back and the chair creaked. "You register him in school?"

"Yes, sir."

He put the papers down. "Miss Williams."

"Yes, sir?"

"Miss Williams, you can look me in the eyes. No one in this office is going to hurt you."

She lifted her gaze and blinked. "I understand, sir."

"And for Christ's sakes stop saying 'sir'. I'm not in the Marines anymore."

She wasn't sure what to say so she nodded as his blue eyes appeared more inquisitive than judgmental. She liked the way a strand of his hair brushed against his forehead, so she quickly glanced away.

Over the last five years she'd grown to hate men. They bullied and pushed and pawed until she couldn't stand the sight or touch of them. So why did she find Sheriff Carter pleasing to look at? She brushed her hand across her forehead. Perhaps she had a fever and was about to come down with something.

Her face felt cool to the touch. *Cora hoped she wasn't blushing.* That's the last thing she needed. To become the sheriff's whore to keep out of trouble. If that happened she wasn't sure what she'd do.

"Have you found a job yet?"

"No. I wanted to wait until Jack started school."

He sat forward, resting his forearms on his desk. "Jobs are mighty scarce around here. Most men can get hired by the mines, a few can find work down at the foundry. It's going to be hard for a woman."

Her jaw tightened and she stared at the wall behind the sheriff. "I know that."

"You ever worked outside the home before?"

She'd been a successful surgeon at a major hospital in St. Louis for four years before being sent to prison, but she was certain that wouldn't matter to him. Besides, she didn't want to have to explain another failure. "Some."

"You have any education?"

She nodded. "Yes."

"They haven't decided on one school teacher yet, but with a record they aren't going to consider you for that. You might try Bart Cooper's dry cleaners, Betty's Diner, and a few other places around town."

"I will. Thank you."

"You have a place to stay?"

"Yes, my aunt, Rose Williams, left me her house."

His face softened. "You were kin to Rose?"

"Yes, sir."

He frowned but a touch of merriment touched his blue eyes. "I thought we had that 'sir' business out of the way."

"I'm sorry." She folded her arms and clutched her elbows. "Habit."

"I understand. But it's a habit you can break now. You're not beholden to anyone. You mind your own business and stay out of trouble, I have no problem with you staying in my county."

"I won't cause any trouble."

"Okay, you can go now." He stood and she immediately jumped to her feet. "I want you to check in with me once a week. Let me know when you get a job and if you have any problems."

She turned to leave. "Thank you, Sheriff Carter."

"No need to thank me. You get yourself back on the straight and narrow and stay there and we'll get along just fine."

She gathered up the papers on his desk, shoved them in the envelope and dashed for the door. She forced herself to slow down before nodding to the deputy and meeting up with Jack outside.

She released a deep breath and wiped the perspiration from her face. Thank God that was over.

"You all done, Aunt Cora?"

Taking his hand, she faked smile. "Yes sweetheart. Let's go home." As they crossed the street curious eyes burned into her back. She didn't know if it was the deputy or the sheriff. Either way, she didn't like it.

***

Virgil Wade stood in the front office staring out the window at Cora Williams and her nephew as they walked toward town. He'd been mistaken about her.

She was a lot prettier than he expected. With big, brown eyes that took up half her face, a pert nose and full mouth with perfect teeth. Her skin was smooth and flawless, with eyelashes that were thick, dark and long. She was petite, yet curvy if she ever got some weight on her. Her hands were small and delicate, yet rough and chapped.

With her looks, there was no way those guards kept their hands off her.

After Ted's phone call, he'd expected her to be harder, meaner and a lot less educated. Instead she'd been humble and obedient. That came from being in prison. He'd seen that fearful gaze a dozen times. Either a person came out pissed off at the world or ready to start a new life.

She wasn't either. Cora Williams was scared to death.

Her hands shook and Virgil knew if he'd said "boo", she'd have flown out of the chair like a cannonball. No doubt she'd been through hell while locked up. Word was prison could be hard on a man, but a lot harder on the female population.

"She's not what I expected," John said, squeezing next to him so he could watch Miss Williams walk away. "Not what I expected at all."

"They rarely are. In this job I've seen all kinds."

"She say what she was in for?"

"No. We didn't talk about that. She's paid her debt. No need to humiliate her."

"I sure hope she doesn't do anything again."

"Yeah, I'd hate to arrest her. I don't know about her kin, but that boy is holding on to her hand like an inner tube in a flood."

"You think anyone will hire her?"

"That's hard to say. I told her to check out Bart's place and the café. Those two have the most turnovers."

"That's cause nobody wants to work for 'em. Bart's a nasty old bastard and they don't call Betty 'The Bitch' for nothing."

"Life's not going to be easy for her no matter where she lives. She did tell me that Rose Williams was her aunt."

"You're shitting me. I really liked Rose."

"We all did. She taught school here for over twenty years."

"I thought she had a brother in St. Louis. You think that's her daddy?"

He shrugged. "Who knows?"

Virgil went back into his office and wished Ted would've left a number with him because he'd like to have a longer conversation with the man. Sitting in his chair, he couldn't help but wonder what all had happened to her behind those gray walls. How had she survived? Things could go really hard for someone as pretty as her. Those guards were half animals at best and no one made them behave themselves.

He promised to find out more when he traveled to Jeff City next week. Until then, he'd keep an eye out for Cora Williams since it appeared no one else in the world cared.

CHAPTER SEVEN

On Tuesday, Cora dropped an excited Jack off at Whitebird Elementary School ten minutes before the bell rang. She hated letting him go but he'd practically pulled her arm out of its socket anxious for his first day.

While he skipped and ran toward the classroom, Cora's stomach churned. They'd only had the Labor Day weekend together before he had to report for school. It seemed unfair. She'd waited so long to get him, only to turn him over to a stranger for the rest of the day.

Resolved to spend time looking for a job, Cora left the school steps and walked back to the downtown area. She planned her first stop to be the dry cleaners. It was an impressive building with large front windows. It sat on the corner of Broadway and Main.

She tried to look into the window but they were too cluttered to make out much. Just as her hand touched the knob, the sheriff's voice carried toward her. "No need to go there until after ten. Bart sleeps in every day."

She jerked and whipped her hands behind her back before turning. She hadn't heard the squad car pull up to the curb. With long powerful strides, Sheriff Carter walked toward her.

"I'll come back later."

He took off his fedora and smoothed the rim with strong hands and lean fingers. "I checked with Betty this morning. She doesn't have anything at the moment."

After swallowing, she licked her dry lips. "Thank you." Unable to stand his scrutiny any longer, she turned to go. "I'll be on my way."

"Miss Williams, there's no call for you to be so skittish."

To avoid his gaze, she watched as several cars made their way down Main Street. Little did he know. Every time she stepped out of the protection of her home, she had a reason to be afraid. Her freedom was the most valuable thing she had and she wanted to protect it as much as possible. "I don't mean to be jumpy. I just don't want any trouble."

"You obey the law and you won't have any."

His words fell on ears that had all too often heard a man's lies about how safe she was. She wouldn't fall for that again. Not as long as she lived.

"I plan to mind my own business and stay out of your way. Now, I'd like to get on with trying to find a job."

His smile slipped and disappointment sparked in his eyes. The realization that she'd been unintentionally rude made her want to apologize. But she couldn't bring herself to do it.

"Sorry to bother you." His voice hinted of regret. He put his hat on, tipped the brim and returned to his car. She heard him drive away as she headed in the opposite direction.

Oh Lord, what had she done? The man was probably only trying to be helpful. The last thing she wanted was to get the attention of the sheriff. That would only be trouble for her and Jack.

Rubbing her hands over her face, she took a few deep breaths then made her way to the drugstore across the street. She knew a lot about medicine. She may not have a license, but that didn't mean she couldn't get a clerk's job or something like that.

She walked up to a young lady sticking price tabs on items across from the soda counter. "Good morning. I'm looking for a job and I was wondering if you're hiring?"

The girl with soft chestnut hair and warm, brown eyes held out her hand. "I'm Caroline Dixon."

Cora accepted the offer. "I'm Cora Williams. My aunt was Rose Williams."

The young lady's pretty eyes lit up. "I loved Miss Rose. She was such a good teacher and a wonderful friend." She tilted her head. "I can see the resemblance."

A blush touched Cora's cheeks. "I'm glad you two were acquainted."

"She and my father knew each other since they were youngsters."

"That's refreshing to know. I live in her house now."

"That's good news. I hated seeing that lovely home abandoned. When did you move here?"

"Four days ago. It's just me and my nephew, Jack."

"We're very happy to have you. Is Jack in school?"

"Yes. This is his first day." Her first real conversation brought relief to her body strung too tight with tension. She was human. She could have a civil chat with a young lady. Cora looked around the store. "Are you doing any hiring?"

The smile slid off her pretty face. "I'm sorry, we're not."

Cora refused to feel sad. "Well, I'm glad I met you, Caroline. If anything comes open will you let me know?" She glanced to the back of the store. "I know a lot about medicine if you ever need help in the pharmacy."

"I'll remember that and tell Mr. Welsh."

"I appreciate it. Thank you, and goodbye."

Caroline waved to her as she stepped out into the autumn air. Several of the leaves on the trees had started turning their fall color. Before long, Christmas would be here. She needed a job.

She visited the mercantile, the office of the Joplin Mining Company, even the funeral home. The hospital at the edge of town beckoned to her like money to the poor. She wanted to enter those doors so badly. To go back to practicing medicine and helping people meant everything to her. But, she had to keep reminding herself that she could never be the woman she was.

Her stomach growled, reminding her she'd only had a piece of toast for breakfast with her coffee this morning. After stopping at the dry cleaners, she planned to go back home for an early lunch.

She entered the store and across the counter stood a woman in her late-forties wearing a print patterned apron. She had long, red hair pulled back and secured at the nape of her neck. She was slim and attractive with a cautious set to her posture. A colored lady stood nearby, close to the same age. She was plump with a face accustomed to smiling. She wore a large, linen apron with a matching bandana. In the back, an elderly woman will into her sixties, skinny and frail, scrubbed clothes. "Is Mr. Cooper here?"

"He's in the office," the lady in the apron said with a troubled gaze. "You need him?"

"I was going to see if he had a job opening."

The employees shared a suspicious glance. "You'd be smart to look somewhere else."

Cora wished she had that luxury. "I need a job and I'll take what I can get."

A plump, balding man walked out of the office, a smelly cigar clamped between his teeth. He wore pants stretched tight around his stomach and a vest that could no longer button. "What's going on here?"

"Mr. Cooper, I came looking for employment."

He squinted his left eye. "You want a job." His hungry eyes devoured every inch of her body. She'd seen that look too many times before. He stepped closer. "I might be hiring."

She didn't say anything. Best she keep quiet and take any job she could get. Jack had to eat and their money would run out soon.

"When can you start?"

"Right now," she replied. However, any enthusiasm of getting a job vanished when she realized what she'd have to do to keep collecting a salary. So, maybe that was why the sheriff recommended she apply here. *Perhaps this is where he thought she belonged.*

Shame heated her whole body and she thought of the lovely lady she'd met at the drugstore. This place didn't have that warm, inviting feel. No, these women were as desperate for work as she was.

"Make it first thing tomorrow morning. Get here at eight and the girls will show you what to do. What's your name?"

"Cora, Cora Williams."

"Okay, Cora Williams, I'll see you tomorrow."

While grateful she'd managed to get a job the first day of looking, that didn't keep her from practically running from the place.

***

Virgil gathered the paperwork he had to take to Jeff City. He'd been dreading the trip, but after the conversation with Ted and meeting Miss Williams, he decided he'd go today. Besides, now he looked forward to visiting Ted.

Running into Miss Williams this morning proved to be troubling. He'd seen her on Main Street and figured she'd been out job hunting. Approaching her had been a mistake.

That woman had some serious fear going on inside her head. He'd worried for a minute that she would faint at the sight of him. He didn't know if it was his size, his badge, or her guilt. And he had no way of telling. He decided to just let her be. Give her some space and see if she settled down.

She kind of reminded him of a skittish colt. Afraid, but not sure what there was to fear. Today she'd worn a nice brown dress, her bobbed hair neatly pinned back and no hint of make-up.

His first impression held up. Cora Williams was one of those naturally beautiful women that rarely comes along. Everything about her appearance from her skin, to her soft autumn-brown eyes to her full mouth, sent out an alluring signal that she was a woman. She barely stood five two and if she weighed a hundred pounds it would surprise him.

Fighting the war as long as he had made a man cultivate the ability to read a person almost the moment their eyes met, and that'd happened with Cora Williams.

He couldn't deny she was probably the prettiest woman he'd ever met. But there was also a lot of sorrow in her, along with fear, disappointment, and loneliness.

Miss Williams had fought her own war.

Determined to find out what he could, Virgil headed north.

A few hours later he shook Ted Young's hand. "You have a moment?"

Ted looked around, nervous as a hen with a fox in the coop. There wasn't a man more occupied with cleanliness then Ted Young. His face and ears gleamed liked he'd buffed them with a shoe shine rag. He had thinning blond hair with brown eyes. His nails were prettier than most women's and his uniform and shoes were spotless.

"Meet me in town. My shift ends in about an hour. There's a diner on the corner of Pine and Sheridan." He gave him a watered-down smile. "I'll buy you a late lunch."

"I'll be there."

Virgil took care of his business and walked into the diner to find Ted waiting for him. After ordering coffee and the daily special, the two men began talking.

"After your phone call, Cora Williams paid me a visit. She's moved into my county and I like to keep close tabs on those fresh out of prison." He took a sip of coffee. "I have to say your call surprised me."

"I just don't want anything to happen to her, that's all."

He had to ask even though he didn't really want to know. "You sweet on her?"

Ted shook his head and Virgil relaxed a little. "Nothing like that. Doc's really a nice gal."

"Doc?"

"Yeah, that's what most of us called her. She was a doctor before she ended up in the slammer."

"You don't say."

"She's a good woman. They put her through hell while she was there, but she toughed it out. Finally, the warden put her in charge of the prison hospital and let it be known she was to be left alone."

"I'll be damned. I didn't know she was a doctor."

"She ain't no more." Ted looked around nervously. "This here is all hearsay between me and you. But, I heard that her daddy is a big businessman with a lot of connections." He winked. "If you know what I mean."

"I reckon I do."

"He made sure she went to prison."

Virgil didn't understand how that could happen. How could a father do that to his daughter? "That's a mean bastard."

"From the bits and pieces, here and there, I've heard he's the meanest."

"What was she in for?"

Eyes darting around the diner, Ted leaned closer and whispered, "Don't know. And neither does anyone else. The paperwork says 'attempted murder', but you and I know a five year sentence doesn't line up with that."

"You're right." Something that serious could get you ten to fifteen easily.

"Nothing makes any sense."

"Is that why you called?"

"Virgil, I've known you since we were kids. You're a good man and I know you'll do the right thing. While Cora was incarcerated, a lot went on in there. Illegal and dangerous stuff."

"You afraid someone might want to shut her up?"

Ted shook his head. "I don't know. But I stuck my neck out to protect her as much as I could."

"How?"

"She wasn't due to be discharged until next month. I fudged the paperwork and released her Thursday while the warden was out of town. I told him and the head guard later that I'd made a mistake."

"You think they might've had something planned?"

Ted plowed his fingers through his hair. "I don't know and I'm not accusing anyone of anything. But, I doubt she'd have lasted another month."

"What about her nephew?"

"Don't know nothing about that. I know she never received a letter or a visitor the whole time she was locked up."

"That's kind of hard."

He whispered. "Yeah, I thought so, too. That's why I finally went to the Warden and explained some of the things going on in the place. I felt someone had to protect her before they killed her and there wouldn't be anyone around to care."

"I take it she had it rough in there."

"You don't even want to know the worst of it. But, she's more than paid her debt to society. She deserves to be left alone and allowed to live in peace. She's a nice woman and the best damn doctor I know."

"Oh?"

"She saved more lives in there than they do in a hospital." He raised his shirt. "Look at that. She took out my appendix."

"That's impressive."

"One of the guards accidently got gut shot by another guard and the doc patched him up and he was just fine."

"I appreciate your information. I'll see she's treated kindly. We're a nice place to live with mostly good people. She'll be fine."

Confusing thoughts ran through his head as he drove back toward Gibbs City. Cora Williams had been a doctor. Few women in today's world could pull something like that off. Becoming a doctor took a lot of schooling and training, not to mention the fight it would take for a woman to survive in a man's place of work.

But, he knew if her father had anything to do with her being locked up, he probably made it where she would never be able to practice medicine again.

Virgil decided he'd do what he could, but he wasn't coddling anyone. She may have proved herself to the prison guard, but she'd yet to do that to him.

CHAPTER EIGHT

Cora went home and fixed a sandwich. When she'd closed the door behind her, vivid memories of some of the meaner guards in prison assaulted her. Bart Cooper had that same look and attitude. He scared the living daylights out of her.

All she had to do was stay out of his reach while she looked for something else. Until then she had little choice. Looking outside, she kicked off her shoes and changed clothes so she could work in the yard.

What an eyesore. Afraid Jack would get hurt by all the junk laying around, she rolled up her sleeves and started working.

Her neighbor, Maggie Cox walked toward her, smiling. "Howdy neighbor"

"Hi Maggie." She tossed several rusted cans into the wheelbarrow. "How are you?"

"I was hoping to see you today." She held out a loaf pan. "I made a coffee cake and thought we'd celebrate the first day of the kids back to school."

"Come in. I'll make coffee."

They sat at the kitchen table. "You did a great job cleaning up this place."

"I didn't." She put the pot on to perk. "Naomi did most of the work."

"That's good. Any luck in the job department?"

"I was hired on at the dry cleaners."

Maggie scooted her chair back and frowned. "Watch Bart. He's pretty handy." Maggie arched a dark brow. "If you know what I mean."

"I can only imagine, but to tell the truth, I didn't have a choice."

"I understand. Sometimes we women have to do what we can to survive. And it ain't always easy."

"You can say that again."

The coffee bubbled and she turned it down to slowly perk. The aroma tickled her nose.

"So, where you from?"

Nervous and afraid because she wanted Maggie to like her, Cora chewed her bottom lip. Could she afford to lose the closest thing to a friend?

"St Louis."

"What are you doing here?"

"Aunt Rose left me her house and I wanted Jack to grow up in a small town."

"No man?"

She shook her head. "Never married."

"Well, it won't be easy."

"I just hope Jack and I can make it."

"Who's child is he?"

"My sister, Eleanor's." Sadness crushed her chest and memories of a beautiful, loving woman touched her thoughts. "She passed."

Maggie reached out and covered her hand. "I'm sorry. I had a brother killed in the war. Nothing's the same after that."

"It's tragic, but I hope we can make it work."

"Lots of folks are struggling. You just have to stay at it."

"I plan to. I can't afford to lose Jack. He means everything to me."

"Just be sure and watch yourself around Bart Cooper. He married into one of the best families in the area, but he's nothing but trash."

"I'll do what I can. But right now, me working determines if we eat."

"Be grateful you have a roof over your head. Virgil just had to evict Paul Anderson's family from their place because they weren't able to keep up the taxes."

"That's a horrible thing to do."

"He didn't have a choice. Believe me if he did, he'd never willingly throw a family out of their home."

"Still, it's sad."

They cut the cake and Cora sat back and listened to Maggie as she brought her up to date on the locals. The sheriff's name was mentioned several times, but she was determined to keep a safe distance.

CHAPTER NINE

Back in Gibbs City, Virgil drove past the house where one of his favorite people used to live. Rose Williams was more than a teacher to him. She'd guided him and had even written him while he served in the Marines. She'd kept him updated on what was happening in his hometown while he was away.

He'd visited her at the nursing home just before she died. She didn't recognize him, but she knew her longtime friend from the colored side of town, Thomas Johnson. The aides at the home said he visited every day. He and his son, JJ.

Virgil slowed the Ford and looked at the weather-beaten house. He wondered how Miss Williams would fare in the county. While the town's folks were hard-working, fair-minded people, he wasn't sure how they'd take to a hardened woman convicted of attempted murder.

Stopping the car, he put it in gear and turned off the key. The engine died and he got out of the automobile and approached the broken steps.

It was mid-afternoon and he heard a noise coming from the back of the house. He went in search of the disturbance and found Cora Williams picking up trash. The old wooden wheelbarrow piled high with junk.

"Afternoon, Miss Williams."

Startled, she screamed and jumped back ten feet. Hands clutched against her chest, eyes wide and already shaking, one would think she'd just robbed a bank.

"Sheriff?"

He removed his hat as he remembered Ted's words. "I didn't mean to scare you."

As if her feet were stuck in a foot of mud, she stood completely still and stared. "What's wrong?"

Ducking his head, he realized there was no reason for him to be here with her. No official business, no news, nothing besides the fact that he just wanted to see her.

So, he resorted to lying. "There's nothing wrong. When you checked in I should've filled out some forms. I need to see your release papers for my files."

"I didn't know you needed that."

"I didn't think about it until you were already gone."

She removed the old work gloves that would come closer to fitting him and had more holes than fabric. Shoving her hair back, she placed the gloves on top of the loaded wheelbarrow and stepped toward the house.

"Shall I get them for you now?"

Virgil felt like a heel. "If it's not too much trouble."

"No, they're inside. Wait a minute and I'll bring them out."

He nodded, but wanted to kick himself for being so conniving. When had he become so eager to see a woman that he was willing to come up with a story that had more holes in it than her screen door?

He watched her go into the house, his conscience chewing him up one side and down the other the whole while. He wanted to be indifferent to her, mind his own business, do his job and protect the county, but what he really wanted was Cora Williams safe.

She came out and held the papers out to him. "There isn't anything wrong is there?"

Fear clouded her eyes and as he looked at the documents, he noticed her hand shaking. *Damn fool, you've gone and scared the living hell out of the woman.* "No, Miss Williams. It's just a formality. Nothing to be concerned about."

"I see."

He hoped she didn't, because she'd see a lying, desperate man who was acting like a schoolboy with his first crush.

"I'll get those forms filled out and return these tomorrow."

"I start working at the dry cleaners tomorrow. Maybe you can just put them in the mailbox."

"Bart gave you a job?"

She chewed her bottom lip and Virgil wanted to tell her not to go to the dry cleaners, to continue looking, that wasn't the place for her. But he had to keep his opinions under wraps. This wasn't any of his business.

"Yes."

"I hope you're able to find something else in the future. I'll keep an ear out should I hear about anything."

"Thank you. That's very kind."

Damn, he felt so bad for her. Standing in the trashed-out yard, living in a house that could fall down around her at any minute, he wondered how she managed. Then there was the child.

A far cry from being a successful doctor.

"I'll stop by after work tomorrow."

Now, what the hell was he doing?

"Okay," she said weakly. "I'll be here."

He put his hat back on and nodded. "Have a nice day, Miss Williams."

"You too, Sheriff."

Back in his squad car, he cranked the engine. What fool-headed idea made him think she wouldn't see right through his feeble excuse to see her? And the big question on his mind was why. He wasn't about to get tangled up with a woman. Especially not someone with all her problems.

He needed to make it a point to avoid her. He'd return the papers tomorrow. Then she wouldn't see him again unless it really was official business.

CHAPTER TEN

After the sheriff left, Cora got busy and cleaned the litter from the yard. She hauled it in a wheelbarrow to the trash yard where other items had been discarded about three blocks away.

In the back right side of her property, covered in weeds, she found the old shed. Inside, there were gardening tools that needed cleaning, a ladder and an old hand plow.

Totally distracted by the visit from the sheriff, Cora was surprised when a man approached walking with a cane. Tall and lean, he had a head of gray hair and a grizzly beard. Wearing coveralls and work boots, he looked grim and determined, maybe even mad.

Oh, Lord.

Using his cane, he pointed to the tall maple tree with its branches hanging over into his yard. "You gotta cut that damn thing down. All the leaves fall in my yard and I gotta pick them up."

Cora shaded her eyes and looked at the massive tree still full of leaves that were just beginning to change to their autumn colors. "I don't think I can do that."

"Well, you better or I'll come out here and chop the whole damn thing down myself."

"Doesn't it offer you a lot of shade in the summer?"

"I don't worry about the summer. It's the gall darn fall that them leaves pile up all over the place."

"I have a rake in the shed. As soon as I get the front yard cleaned up, my nephew and I'll make sure you don't have to put up with leaves."

"That won't do no good. You know how many leaves I get?"

"I have no idea. But it's the only solution I can offer at this time."

"You need to get someone to cut down that tree."

"I don't want to do that." Realizing they hadn't introduced themselves, she extended her hand. "I'm your neighbor, Cora Williams."

He didn't take her hand. Instead, he narrowed one eye and leaned closer. "You kin to Rose?"

"She was my aunt."

"You living here now?"

"Yes. She was kind enough to leave it to me."

"Ain't seen you around these parts."

"I was away. I lived in St Louis."

"And no time to visit a poor ailing relative?"

"I've been here on many occasions." She lowered her head unable to meet the man's gaze. "I'm the little girl whose footprints are in your sidewalk."

He straightened quickly as the memory must've danced through his mind. "Humph, you were nothing but trouble then and probably still are."

"I apologized."

"That didn't fix my sidewalk."

"But I never imagined my prints would stay there permanently."

"What'd you expect?" He shouted, again raising his cane. "It was cement."

She hunched her shoulders. "But I didn't know that."

"You're gonna keep my yard clean of leaves and behave yourself or I'll take this walking stick to you."

"Yes, sir."

The old man Aunt Rose had referred to as Satan himself, was actually Earl Clevenger. And he and her aunt had argued for years. Never could get along. Once, while she and Eleanor were there for a summer visit, Aunt Cora threw a bucket of wash water in his face.

And the battle roared on.

Checking the time, she realized Jack would be out of school soon and she needed to be waiting there for him should he get lost. Walking through town she saw Caroline from the drugstore. The young woman sent a friendly wave and smiled. Cora wondered how long that would last once word got out she was a felon.

Passing Howard Martin's Grocery, she crossed the street to glance into the window of the dry cleaners where she'd be working tomorrow. The place made her skin crawl and shiver. What she wouldn't give to have another job lined up, but she didn't and she and Jack had to survive. For him, she'd do anything.

The air turned chilly, but in a good way and she found the walk exhilarating and her spirits lifted. She and Jack had a roof over their heads and freedom to do as they pleased without a guard standing over them every minute of the day, egging them on only to beat them silly.

Her freedom was complete and, although there would only be enough money for food and utilities, contentment filled her chest and her steps lightened.

At the school, she waited until she saw Jack barreling downing the steps, a wide grin on his face. "I had so much fun today."

"Do you like your teacher?"

"Miss Potter is real nice. I have my own desk."

"That's wonderful." Tommy fell in beside them. Several kids ran and scrambled to play on the way home. The sight cheered her heart and gave her hope. Ah, to be young and free again.

Just as they crossed Main Street the familiar black and white sheriff's car drove by slowly. Inside the coupe, Sheriff

Carter touched the brim of his hat and she wondered if he was watching her. God forbid she go to the bank. He'd probably suspect her of robbing the place.

At home, Jack changed into his play clothes and hit the back screen door, anxious to join his newly found friends. She took out a chicken to fry for dinner and enjoyed the idea of making a meal for her and Jack because they were a family.

Except for Eleanor, she'd never had that in her life.

As she looked around their house, she felt quite pleased with the way things were. The furniture was older than sin, but comfortable. The rug needed to be replaced, but it was good enough for now. They had to get a new stove soon because only two burners worked and the oven was as temperamental as a mule.

The whole concept felt strange. In her life before prison she had a career and more money than she could spend, then nothing, now Jack.

She'd have to save up for extras. Not wanting to even think what they would cost her, she rolled the meat in flour and turned on the burner under the cast iron skillet. After putting a glop of lard in to melt, she salted and peppered the chicken.

Next she set about peeling potatoes with a small paring knife so dull you could barely cut warm butter, but somehow she managed to chop the potatoes to boil.

Thirty minutes later, she called Jack in to wash up for supper. The sweet boy was so excited to have friends to play with and attend school, he chattered all through dinner. "I like your fried chicken."

"I'm glad," she replied. "We'll probably be eating a lot of it."

"Good."

When she cleaned off the kitchen table and Jack sat down to read, she noticed the police car again. But he drove by and stopped at the house down the street. She opened the window above the kitchen sink so she could hear what was happening. Sheriff Carter seemed to be on official business and he didn't look happy.

"Warren," the sheriff called out loudly. "You come out here."

A tall, lanky man with wild hair and a straggly beard barreled out of a weathered, dilapidated house wearing baggy, stained pants with suspenders over his grimy undershirt. "I ain't done a damn thing wrong."

"Teacher says otherwise. Ronnie went to school today with marks on him. I've warned you."

"He's my damn kid and I'll do what I want."

"You keep this up and the State will take him away."

"I don't give a shit."

"He's your son."

"He ain't nothing but a pain in the ass."

"You better keep your hands to yourself or I'll lock you up."

"For what? Whipping my own kid?"

"Because I don't like a man who beats a child."

Jack asked, "What's going on, Aunt Cora?"

"I guess the sheriff is paying a visit to one of our neighbors." She heard a chair scrape across the linoleum floor.

Soon, Jack stood beside her, his hands propped on the window sill. "That's Ronnie. Miss Potter took him to the principal's office this morning. But I don't think he did anything wrong."

The idea that a man like the sheriff stood up for a child impressed her, yet she'd never admit it. After all, he was the law and she knew what they were capable of.

It appeared he was a man who did the right things for the right reasons. Mistreating a child was a horrible situation. As a doctor she'd seen plenty of kids beaten and maimed, some even died from injuries inflicted by their parents. Laws should be made to protect children.

Looking closer, she noticed a young, ragged little boy a little smaller than Jack, hiding behind the porch pillar. He looked scared to death and the way he cowered, he'd been abused more than once. She hoped the sheriff didn't make things worse by challenging his father.

Poor thing.

The sheriff flew up the stairs and knocked the man down on the porch. He stood over him, his fists clenched. "You hurt that boy again and I'll put you behind bars for as long as the law will allow."

He turned and went to his car, reached in and pulled out some papers then walked toward her house.

CHAPTER ELEVEN

After being sorely tempted to shoot Warren Hayes, Virgil took Cora Williams' papers he'd received from her that afternoon and walked a few doors down to her house.

After a day of mentally scolding himself for acting like a lovesick puppy, he decided to stick to his decision to avoid her. He made his way to the front and up the broken stairs.

Two knocks and she cracked the door. Virgil removed his hat and handed her the papers he'd lied about earlier. "Thank you."

The little boy squeezed between him and Miss Williams. "Hi, Sheriff."

Virgil knelt down and shook the child's hand. "Howdy. My name is Sheriff Carter. What's yours?"

"Jack. My name is Jack. I go to school, too."

"You like it?"

"Yeah, it's fun."

"That's a good boy."

"We saw you punch that man. You really hit hard."

Virgil looked up at Miss Williams and a worried frown and sad eyes made him ashamed he'd lost his temper. "I'm sorry about that."

Jack made a fist and punched the air. "You should've gave him a black eye. Jimmy Martin, a kid in my class has a black eye."

"Well, knowing Jimmy the way I do, he probably got that by aggravating his older brothers. He's an ornery little cuss."

The boy laughed. "That's what Miss Potter said."

Miss Williams put her hand on Jack's shoulder. "You need to get ready for bed. Besides, I'm sure the sheriff is busy."

"I'll leave now."

Jack took off back into the house.

She looked at him. "Did you get everything you need?"

"Yes."

"Everything's in order?"

"It is."

Apparent relief had her letting go of a deep breath. "Good, I don't want to do anything wrong."

"You're fine."

"Good night, Sheriff."

"Wait a minute."

She stepped closer. "Something else?"

"No," he replied, tightening his lips. "If you have any trouble with Bart, just let me know."

"I'm sure I'll be fine. But, thank you anyway."

After leaving the Williams' house, Virgil decided to drive out to see his folks. Guilt chewed at him because he hadn't been by in a few days to check and see how they were doing. It wasn't a visit he looked forward to but, as the last of their children, he felt obligated.

His father opened the door then went back to his favorite chair and lowered the volume of the radio. No doubt they were listening to a show. Now, in their late sixties, one would think they were both ready for the grave.

The spark of life had deserted them when two of their sons were killed in the war. There was no happy reunion when Virgil returned, only regrets that the other two hadn't made it home.

They mourned the loss of their two sons while he carried the guilt that he was the lucky one to return. He didn't know why, by all accounts he should've been dead a dozen times. But he lasted through it all.

His oldest brother, James, was killed on the USS Arizona in Pearl Harbor. Sam, the youngest, died in Europe during the Battle of the Bulge. Neither body made it home for a burial.

After the war, Virgil just wanted to come home and be safe and not have anyone shooting at him. The loving arms of his parents should've been his refuge. Instead, they'd suffered so much heartbreak it was like they'd stopped loving him for fear they couldn't endure any more pain.

Now, in the house where he'd been raised, he felt like a complete stranger.

"Evening, Dad." While his father sat in the chair, his mother chose her rocker and continued knitting. Virgil sat at the end of the green divan. "How are you doing today?"

"We're fine." His father picked up his pipe and packed it with tobacco. He struck a match to fire up his favorite pipe. The one Virgil had bought him for Christmas last year.

"I thought I'd check and see if you needed anything from the store or if there's anything else I could do to help out."

"No, your mom and I walked to Martin's the other day."

"You know, I don't mind helping out around here."

"We know that, but don't want you to bother. We can manage."

"I know you can, but you don't need to. I'm your son and I'll gladly take you for a few errands."

"We can manage. Your mom is worried about winter. She always gets sick during the cold. Can't hardly stand it."

She pulled a shawl she knitted around her shoulders. "I shiver from October to April."

"You plan on putting in a garden next spring?"

"Too much trouble." His dad rubbed his lower back. "My old bones act up and I can't hardly move."

"Why don't you go to the doctor?"

"Oh, those quacks don't know a damn thing."

His mother put down her handiwork. "All they do is peddle pills. Got a pill for every ailment there is."

"I noticed you haven't been in church the last few Sundays."

"I ain't going until Preacher Fuller stops talking about giving more money to the church. We give what we can and all he does is stand up there and preach about giving more. Well, dammit, I've done my share."

"What about you, Mom? You and your friends still play cards?"

"No, not since Wanda had her gallbladder taken out. She's been puny ever since."

His dad stood. "I'm getting me a cup of coffee. You want one."

"No thanks. I just came by to check on you."

His dad took a puff on his pipe. "You don't need to do that. We ain't dead yet."

Sadness wrapped around his heart like a worn-out blanket. Nothing would ever be the same and yet nothing would ever change. "I don't mean to imply that. I just want to see you. You are my parents or have you forgotten you still have one son."

"We had three before the damn war."

Virgil walked out. There was no getting past all the bitterness his folks felt about losing their other two sons.

He got in his squad car and headed back to the office to do some paperwork. Maybe he'd stop by and see Frank at the fire station. He went out of his way to drive past Cora Williams' house. A warm light spilled from the window over the kitchen sink and he figured the boy had been put to bed and maybe she sat at the table reading or enjoying a cup of coffee.

The rest of the house remained dark. As he pulled up to the corner, he noticed she sat on the dark porch with a cup cradled in her hands looking up at the stars. He wanted to pull over, but he didn't dare. She had to make it on her own and he didn't want the tongues wagging.

He drove on.

At the station he turned on the lights and walked into his deputy's area and on to his office. The paperwork from Miss Williams lay on his desk. He picked it up and studied it briefly. So few words to sum up so much.

To the right of his desk was a door that concealed the tiny room he lived in. There was only a cot, a tiny dresser, a rack to hang his uniforms on, a shoe shining kit in the corner and a hot plate. There was a toilet with a sink for him to shave and a mirror above it.

It was bare and sparse because the city paid for it and they didn't believe in luxuries. He could live at his parents, but he wouldn't be able to deal with their constant sorrow. He'd once thought of buying a house, but decided he didn't want to bother. Besides, his little room was bigger than a foxhole.

The sheriff before him had been married and the room was used for storage. When he accepted the job and left his father's filling station, he cleaned out all the junk and made himself at home. If a person wanted to call it that.

Earlier he'd stopped at Betty's Diner for supper then he spent some time with Frank at the fire station, now there wasn't anything for him to do but think.

Later that night, with the town quiet and most of the businesses closed, Virgil washed up for bed. Sitting on the edge of the cot, he took off his dress shoes and his socks. He realized for the last six years he'd never seriously thought about a woman until Cora Williams came to Gibbs City.

CHAPTER TWELVE

The next day, after dropping Jack off at school, Cora opened the door of Bart Cooper's Dry Cleaning and Laundry Service and stepped into her new job. The taller woman close to her age met her at the counter. "You here to work?"

"Yes."

She swung the hinged counter up and Cora followed her to the back of the store. "I'm Helen White. I been working here four years. I'm not really the boss, but sometimes Bart asks me to tell you all what to do."

"Okay. My name is Cora Williams."

The black woman, round as a washtub stepped closer. "You kin to Rose?"

"She was my aunt."

"Well, I'll be. You looks like her."

"Thank you."

"My name is Nellie, but you can call me Nell. Most people do."

Helen pointed to an elderly woman bent over a steamy washtub filled with clothes. "That's Pearl Baker. We call her Ma Baker cause she's older than the hills around here."

Ma Baker held up a wooden paddle. "I ain't too old to whop you in the head with this stick."

Helen walked away. "She gets a little riled, but she don't mean no harm."

"I understand." Cora looked around and wondered if Bart had ever heard about modern washers and dryers. It was 1947 after all. Even her aunt had a Maytag washing machine.

Helen put her hand on Cora's shoulder. "You need to watch yourself around here."

Nell stood within hearing distance and nodded somberly.

Helen continued, "Old man Cooper is a mean bastard and he expects a lot from his employees. If you want to keep working you don't say nothing and just do what you're told."

"I need a job."

"Pretty thing like you should be able to do better than this."

"I took what I could get."

"Okay, come over here and I'll show you what to do."

Cora wanted to do a good job and hoped she'd be able to stay but only until something better came along. She learned in a matter of minutes that she would be the main ironer and the counter clerk for the customers. If she finished the ironing, she had to help the others. No one stood around doing nothing.

She was at the counter waiting on a Mrs. Collinsworth when Bart came in. He smiled at his customer and asked about her family. Then he turned and went to his office and shut the door. When Cora glanced at the other women, a notable difference had come over the shop.

Everyone worked harder and no one spoke a word. As she went back to ironing sheets, Bart finally came out. "I wasn't sure you'd show up."

She put the iron on the metal pad. "I'm here, sir."

"Around here everyone pulls their own weight or they're fired." He moved closer and put his finger close to her nose. "And you keep your mouth shut about what goes on in this place, you hear?"

"Yes, sir."

"Don't go giving me no call to fire you, cause I will, girl. I want all of you working your asses off."

The bell above the door chimed and Bart's demeanor completely changed. Smiling like a kid with candy, he stretched out his hand as he moved toward the counter. "Why, Reverend Fuller, how nice to see you."

"Thank you, Bart. The church is in need of your help and since you're a Deacon I thought I'd come to you first."

Bart's smile deepened. "What do you need?"

"We want someone to head the committee for the needy. Ester would be perfect for the position."

Bart clasped the preacher's hands. "I'll ask her tonight at supper. I'm sure she'll agree. She's such a compassionate woman."

"She is indeed."

"Anything else, Reverend?"

"No, I'll be on my way." He tipped his hat. "You ladies have a lovely day."

Bart turned around and stomped to his office and slammed the door so hard the sign with the prices for dry cleaning fell off the wall. Nell quickly picked it up and hung it back on the nail.

Cora didn't know what that was all about, but one thing was clear, Bart wasn't the nice guy he pretended to be around customers. She kept at the ironing until she thought her arm would fall off. Soon, Helen came over and tapped her on the shoulder.

"Time for lunch."

Cora eyed the counter. "What about the customers?"

"We eat over there." She pointed to a small square table with four wooden chairs. Earlier it'd been stacked with folded clothes, now it was cleared off for them to eat. "From there we all keep an eye out and we can hear the bell."

Cora had brought a peanut butter and jelly sandwich. She didn't want to dip into Jack's lunch supplies. He needed those for school. But she had put a carrot in her lunch should the sandwich not fill her.

She sat at the table. Nell took a jug of iced tea from an old beat-up refrigerator and they drank out of Mason fruit jars. "Why was Bart so mad at the preacher?"

Ma Baker looked around. "They don't like each other. 'Sides, Bart thinks that Preacher Fuller thinks his wife is more important than him."

"That seems a little silly."

Nell took a sip of her tea. "He's a mean, spiteful man who married Miss Ester because her daddy had money. He's been waiting years to get his hands on it, but the old man ain't even close to dying."

They'd been sitting less than twenty minutes when Bart stormed out of his office. "Get your asses to work. I don't pay you to sit around."

Without a single word, everyone jumped and returned to what they'd been doing earlier. No one looked him in the eye and no one murmured a sound.

He jammed his hat on his head. "I'm going to lunch. I'll be back later." He pointed to Helen. "Keep working. I got no patience for lollygaggers."

When the door closed, Nell wiped her brow. "Thank the Good Lord, he's gone for a few hours."

Cora wet her finger and tested the heat of the iron. "We don't get but a few minutes for lunch and he takes hours?"

"He ain't just going to lunch," Helen admitted. "He'll be paying a certain woman a visit before the day's over."

Cora knew what that implication meant and she had no intention of getting caught up in gossip. Instead she turned back and continued ironing even though her shoulders ached and her feet hurt. By the time Bart returned from lunch, he wasn't in a better mood and she smelled the booze on his breath from across the room. She kept her eyes on her business and her mouth shut.

When she helped Pearl hang sheets outside, she noticed that Bart spent most of his day in the back, out by a shed. She'd seen several men come by to talk to Bart. Why was he not doing business inside?

Bart was standing at the counter when the sheriff came in. Cora immediately averted her gaze, but that didn't stop her heart from racing or her hands from trembling.

All the women working called out a friendly hello and he replied. That wasn't unusual because, according to Helen, Bart wanted them all to be nice to their customers and call them by name.

"You got a minute, Bart?"

"I do, Sheriff. Is anything wrong?"

"Just a few words." Sheriff Carter nodded to Bart's office then he lifted up the counter and followed the owner. They went into the office and closed the door.

Cora worried the conversation could be about her. What if he told Bart she was a felon, an ex-con who could be trouble? She blinked back tears. She needed this job.

Helen came over and put her arm across her shoulders. "You don't need to worry about Sheriff Carter. He's a good man."

Nell came over and picked up a spool of black thread. "'Sides, Bart is into a lot of stuff. My guess is the sheriff's here about something Bart's done wrong."

Everyone jumped when the door opened and hurried back to their work. She was glad her back was to the sheriff when he walked through the shop. Bart was right behind him.

"You need to remember who's on the town council."

She dared a look over her shoulder as the sheriff turned. "You need to remember I don't work for the town. I work for the county and I'm here on Judge Garner's behalf."

Cora frantically moved the iron back and forth over the shirt she was ironing. She tried to make herself look as small as possible. Old memories flooded her mind. She hunched her shoulders, expecting a smack across her back.

The blow didn't come, but Bart was so mad she feared he'd strike out at someone and she didn't want that to be her. Luckily for all of them, after the sheriff left, Bart had company. Helen said it was his wife. She pranced in like a princess.

Cora turned as the attractive woman and her daughter smiled at Bart and kissed his cheek. She wanted to vomit. Didn't the woman realize what a no-gooder he was?

"Bart, darling, Alice and I have just returned from Joplin and we couldn't find a thing for the gala."

"That's too bad, dear. You'll just have to keep looking. I'm sure the perfect ensemble is out there."

Mrs. Cooper took off her long gloves and straightened her hat. "I'm sure you're right." She looked at Cora. "Who's this?"

"A new girl to work the counter. Business is getting better." He tickled his wife's chin. "You know I insist on giving our customers the best service available."

His words were sweeter than pure cane syrup.

"Of course you do." She offered her hand to Cora. "My name is Ester and this is my daughter, Alice."

"Very pleased to meet you, ma'am."

Alice twisted a strand of her hair. "I hope you enjoy working for my daddy. He's the nicest man in the whole town."

Cora wanted to roll her eyes and speak up, but the cautious looks on the other women's faces made her smile and agree.

"Well, we must be going. I'll see you at dinner tonight."

"Goodbye, dear."

After they left, Cora exchanged puzzled looks with the other workers who simply shrugged. Did no one but them know the real Bart?

And poor Alice. She was such a plain young girl and it didn't seem there was much hope of her growing out of the awkward stage. Bucked teeth, round, fat face marred with pimples, and hair like baling wire. The poor girl didn't stand a chance.

The day went well and she was glad for the time of year. This place could become very hot in the dead of summer.

Helen came by and told her she'd fit in very well. "You do good work. But you have to watch the boss. He'll paw all over you if you let him. And don't mess with him in the afternoon. He's mean as a snake."

Cora picked up her purse and waved goodbye to the other women. "See you tomorrow."

The dry cleaner was one of the first businesses to close for the day. Helen told her it was because Bart didn't trust anyone and guarded his money like he was afraid someone would try to steal from him. He always rushed to the bank daily before it closed.

Reminding herself that all this was for Jack, Cora hurried to the school to find him standing with Tommy and little Ronnie.

CHAPTER THIRTEEN

Virgil went back to the station to find John thumbing through some old posters. "You get Adeline on the bus to Joplin?"

"Yes, and she called her folks and told them that she was coming."

"Good." Virgil hung his hat up. "Did you give her the money I left for her?"

"Yes, I told her she should be thankful." He put the posters away. "What did Bart have to say?"

"That piece of shit denied the whole thing. Claims he didn't go near her."

John rose and went to the little counter where the hot plate sat and refilled his coffee cup. "Well, by God, someone beat her up."

"We both know Bart's guilty as hell." Virgil hated a man putting his hands on a woman, especially one so young. Adeline was barely out of her teens and here that jackass was having sex with her and slapping her around at the same time. "I wish she would have pressed charges. Nothing would make me happier than putting his ass behind bars. Although, I think I put the fear of God into him."

"I can't understand for the life of me why old man Bridges puts up with that cheesy butthole."

"For one thing, Bart's married to the man's daughter and he never was one to raise a ruckus."

"Yeah, but he can't keep hiding what a no account SOB he has in his family."

"He will if he knows what's good for him. Ester ever leaves him, he's got nothing."

John took a sip of his coffee and puckered his lips. "I reckon you're right. He was always a no account before he married her."

"I always wondered what she saw in him."

"I found it strange he never went into the service. Spent the whole war safe at home."

Virgil hadn't thought of that. John was too young, but those over eighteen were called up at one time or another. Yet Bart somehow got out of serving. "Maybe he didn't pass the physical."

John sat down, his brow furrowed. "That don't seem right. The man appears healthy to me."

"We don't know, so let's not go guessing. But, I'm keeping my eye on him."

"Did that Williams woman get a job there?"

"Yes, I saw her when I talked to Bart."

"I hope she can handle herself around him."

"I checked at several other businesses but there wasn't anything promising."

"Let's just hope that since Bart doesn't have Adeline to beat up anymore, he won't turn to Miss Williams."

"He knows I won't let him get away with that."

"Say, I saw her over the weekend with a little boy. Was she married?"

"No husband. It appears she's raising her nephew, Jack. When she enrolled him in school, she put down that she was his legal guardian."

"Hum, that's strange."

"We need to be careful and keep out of her business. She's skittish around the law. Best if we give her room to live her life."

"When I drove by the park Saturday she had the boy out there playing with the Cox boys and the kid seemed happy as a lark."

Virgil had made a point to check on her every day. As a matter of fact, he easily could've talk to Bart when he saw him going into Betty's diner. Instead, he waited for him to go back to work so he'd have the opportunity to see Miss Williams.

He didn't want to frighten her, but she could so easily become Bart's next victim because of her fear of doing anything wrong. After all these years of being alone, Virgil felt a strong need to protect her. That might not be natural and he didn't think for one minute she would be interested in messing with him, but he couldn't deny how he felt.

Cora Williams needed a champion and he wanted to be there if she needed help. Didn't that beat all? Here he'd always figured he'd be a bachelor all his life and now he had a strong urge to have a home instead of a cot in a storage room.

CHAPTER FOURTEEN

After a full week of work, Cora looked forward to the weekend. Helen took off Wednesdays to be with her mother. That meant Helen ran the store until noon on Saturdays.

Jack rose early his first day off from school and, after breakfast, headed outdoors to play. She watched from the front room as he darted across the street towards Maggie Cox's house to find Tommy.

An inner peace surrounded her knowing that Jack was happy and healthy and more importantly, he'd made a friend. Soon she saw the boys in a mock sword fight with sticks. She worried they might accidently poke out an eye, but then boys would be boys. What kind of life would Jack have if she were over-protective? Little Ronnie, who Cora guessed was a year younger than Jack and Tommy, stood nearby cheering them on. Miss Potter taught the first, second and third grades in one classroom.

She stayed busy with cleaning and laundry. While she had a washing machine, clothes still had to be hung on the clothesline. Thankfully, the sun was out and a gentle breeze blew. Come winter, clothes would be strung all over the house to dry.

While she was outside dealing with laundry, Maggie came by. "I see it's Saturday morning cleaning."

Cora stopped and turned. "Yes, I want to get everything done today so tomorrow after church I can relax a little."

"How'd it go with old Bart the fart?"

She closed her eyes and shook her head. "That man is such a phony. He's sweet as pie in front of the customers and his wife, but behind their backs, he's a disgusting hypocrite."

Maggie stuck her hands in the pockets of her apron and laughed. "That don't surprise me none. Never did care for that man."

"He's horrible. I hope I can find something else soon. I'm really dreading payday next Friday."

Maggie rolled her eyes and her cheeks turned pink. "If even half the rumors I hear are true, you'd be smart to run for the hills."

Wringing her hands, she averted her gaze. "I can't. I need the money."

"Then you need to head for the hills."

"I can't do that, Maggie." Sweat peppered her skin and she shivered. "I just can't."

"Then tell him to leave you alone and threaten to go to Sheriff Carter. That'll make him behave."

"Then he'll fire me."

Maggie released a weary breath. "You're right." Her neighbor turned and pointed. "Look, there's the sheriff now."

Cora turned away. She didn't want to encourage him to stop. He made her as nervous as Bart, only in a different way. He wore a badge. She cringed when a car door slammed. Picking up a pair of Jack's britches, she clipped them to the line and hoped Maggie would go to him instead of him coming to them.

She didn't get her wish.

"Morning, Maggie," he said in a deep voice that touched a soft spot in her chest. "Morning, Miss Williams."

She turned and saw he'd removed his hat and his dark blond hair shined in the sunlight.

After a moment, she lowered her gaze and folded her arms. "Sheriff."

"Howdy, Virgil. How you doing?"

"I'm good, thank you. I'm out and about checking on a few things."

"I figured you be at your folks' today."

"I'll stop by there later."

"I guess you and Cora have met since you knew her name."

"Yes, we've met. How are you? I saw where you got a job at the dry cleaners."

"Yes, sir."

He narrowed his eyes in a polite warning.

"I mean, yes."

Satisfied she got the hint about the "sir" business, he nodded. "Good. Do you like it?"

"Shoot no, she don't like working for that scalawag." Maggie crunched up her face. "Nobody does."

"You have any other prospects."

She pressed her lips together and shook her head.

"Hey, what about Harriet's job at the bank?" Maggie asked. "She's retiring and plans to move to Baxter Springs, Kansas to live near her sister. Maybe old man Kerr at the bank will hire her? Cora here is real smart."

Cora and Virgil's eyes clashed for an instant. They both knew no bank would ever hire a convicted felon. Her stomach tightened and her breath caught in her chest.

"I stopped by there and I think he already has someone in mind."

She let out a breath and her shoulders relaxed. She highly suspected he was fibbing, but was grateful just the same.

"Thank you," she managed to say then went back to her laundry.

"I'll let you know if I hear of anything."

He put on his hat and turned toward his police car. His strides were sure and confident. Those of a man who did the right thing. She imagined he'd never broken the law.

"Virgil sure is a nice fella. Known him all my life." She waved when he got in the squad car and looked back. "That man needs a wife."

"He isn't married?"

Maggie grinned and nudged her with her arm. "No, you interested?"

"Absolutely not." Cora went back to hanging up her clothes, thankful that her undergarments were still inside soaking.

"He sure is a looker."

Cora tightened her lips and concentrated on her task. "I hadn't noticed."

When she stole a look at Maggie, she raised her brow giving her a skeptical look. "Every other single woman in this town has. Single or married."

In church the next morning, Cora and Jack sat in the middle of the small, clapboard church and listened to Minister Charles Fuller. Jack sat next to her swinging his feet, bored to tears. She knew it would be hard for him to remain quiet, so she reached in her pocket and held out a piece of peppermint candy. His eyes lit up and a toothless grin split his face.

The sermon was on turning the other cheek. Cora held little hope in that kind of nonsense. Good way to get the snot beaten out of you.

Maggie and Helen introduced her to several of the local ladies and they asked her to join the Women's Prayer Committee, and they were welcoming, but Cora knew that could be temporary. She loved the little town but she dreaded when the time came for the citizens to learn the truth about her past.

After church, Cora sent Jack off to change into his play clothes while she packed a picnic lunch. They had leftover chicken, pickles, bread she'd baked last night and a can of peaches. She stirred together a pitcher of iced tea. Lemonade would've been wonderful, but much too pricy for her pocketbook.

Holding Jack's hand in one of her hands and the basket in the other, they walked two blocks to the local park. Under a large oak tree Jack tried to spread out a light blanket while she unloaded their goodies and set out the plates.

The weather was beautiful but she knew it wouldn't be long until winter set in and days like this would be rare. Gibbs

City didn't get as cold or as much snow as St Louis, but it did have four seasons. Just as they finished eating and she'd put away the remainder of their lunch, Sheriff Carter stepped over to them.

She jumped when he came from behind. "Hi there, Jack."

Jack grinned, flashing the empty space between his front teeth. "Howdy, Sheriff."

He knelt down to where he and Jack were at eye level.

Jack pointed to the badge pinned to the man's khaki shirt. "Does that make you the sheriff?"

Carter nodded. "It's a symbol of law enforcement."

"If you took it off would you still be the sheriff."

"I would."

Her nephew pointed to the sheriff's waist. "Is that a gun?"

"Yes, it is?"

"Can I hold it?"

"No!" Cora grabbed Jack by the shoulders. "No, Jack. Guns are dangerous."

"Listen to your aunt. She's right."

Jack turned as Tommy walked toward them. He shook hands with the sheriff and ran off to play.

"He's a fine boy."

"You know I have legal custody of him."

"I'd never challenge that. It's clear to see you love that boy."

She gazed at her lap. "I never want to lose him."

"You're safe here, Cora. You need to realize that."

Being here alone with the sheriff made her discomfort grow, but she couldn't get up and walk away. She didn't want to anger him either.

In the distance, a man called out. "Hey, Virgil Wade, it's your turn."

He stood and touched the brim of his hat. "I have a game of horseshoes waiting for me. You enjoy the rest of your afternoon."

Grinning, he joined several other men. Four stood at one end and four at the other. She hadn't watched a game like that in years. It brought a smile to her face.

She glanced over at Jack and Tommy. Two other boys had come up with a ball, they all ran around laughing and shouting as they tried to get it over a ragged old net.

In a box in the closet, Cora had discovered a book. She had brought it along with them. Relaxing, she flipped the pages wishing days like today would never end.

But, of course, people didn't know she hid behind a lie. Once the truth was known, her days as an acceptable resident would be over and done with.

CHAPTER FIFTEEN

Seeing Cora at the park with her nephew pulled hard at Virgil's feelings. He couldn't help but wish that he had his own family, maybe even a son. Something and someone to belong to. He'd much rather have sat on the blanket with her than finish the game with a few of the men from town.

Maggie had invited him for lunch and she didn't stop talking about Cora. He had a pretty strong feeling his old friend was playing Cupid. He didn't know how he felt about that. But, Cora had made it clear she was scared half to death of him or probably anyone representing the law.

Better he mind his own business. He'd be foolish to make a pass at her. He must be getting sappy in his old age. Mostly he figured he was probably lonely. He'd never really had a woman he thought enough of to want to marry. Yet, since Cora Williams came to town, he wanted more out of life than a tiny room.

Virgil stopped at the fire station and saw Frank out wiping down the new shiny truck. Council had finally let go of the money to replace the old one that didn't run half the time.

"What's up, Frank?"

"Oh, not much and I'm hoping it stays that way." Frank was their only official fireman. Most of the other men in the county were volunteers. When a fire happened, the whole town turned out.

He looked at the sky. "Yeah, won't be long and old man winter will come rolling in and everyone turns on their new furnaces." That was the number one cause of most fires in the area, that and space heaters.

"I've gone to a few of the older folks and made sure theirs were working properly, but one never knows."

Frank's wife walked out wiping her hands on a dishrag. "Hey there, Virgil."

"Hey yourself, Mae. How're you doing?"

"Glad it's Sunday."

"Hospital keeping you busy?"

"Worse than ever."

He leaned against the fire pole. "Didn't you start your nursing in St Louis?"

"Yes, at St Louis General."

He shoved his hat back. Mae was the know-it-all in town. What she didn't know, she'd find out soon enough. "Did you happen to meet a doctor named Cora Williams?"

"Sure, she was the only woman doctor in the state."

"What'd you think of her?"

Mae put down the dish towel and cocked her head. "Well, I didn't know her real well, but I saw her once in a while at the hospital."

"She any good?"

Mae lifted her brows. "Oh, yeah. She was a damn good surgeon." She twisted her mouth in disgust. "None of the men doctors liked hearing that, of course. But, I heard she was smart as a whip and really nice to work with."

If she had such a great future, he wondered why she'd do something foolish enough to get thrown in the joint. Maybe it was a lover's quarrel. Crazier things happened between a man and a woman than what went on in bed.

Mae looked into the distance. "I later heard she'd been offered a position at a hospital in another state. She must've taken it because she just disappeared." She glared at him. "Why you asking, Virgil?"

"She's moved to town."

Mae's eyes widened and she stepped closer. "She gonna be working at the hospital?"

"No, I don't think so."

"Well, why not?"

"You'll have to ask her."

Mae turned to go inside. "You have the tightest lips in the county. A body can't get a word out of you unless they reach down your throat and pull it out."

He chuckled. "See ya later."

Frank grinned. "You always could get a rise out of her."

"That's because I teased her all through grade school."

Virgil left the fire station and went to his small room and washed up. He usually went to his folks' place on Sunday. Sometimes they waited dinner, other times they didn't bother. At least if he didn't have to eat, he could leave sooner.

CHAPTER SIXTEEN

Jack finally wore himself out and they decided to go home. He still had to have a bath and get ready for school the next day. Holding her hand, he talked his head off until they arrived home.

From inside his pocket he pulled out two, plastic green army men and turned on the radio to listen to a popular kid's cowboy program that aired on Sunday nights.

Yesterday she'd picked up several apples from the yard that had fallen from Mr. Clevenger's tree. Taking a few others from the branches that leaned over her fence, she started peeling.

Watching Jack, she decided to surprise him with a pie since they'd be having sandwiches for dinner. With the pastry in the oven and his show nearly over, Cora washed dishes and listened as the small town settled down. Crickets chirped and a dog barked in the distance. Inside her home, contentment seemed to pour from the walls, encircling her and Jack in a blanket of security.

Times like this, Cora tried to push all her problems away. To not think about payday, or finding another job, or Maggie learning the truth. Not even the sharp blue eyes of Sherriff Carter.

Just before bedtime, she and Jack paid their neighbor a visit. She knocked while Jack, grinning, held the warm pie.

Mr. Clevenger opened the door with a sour look on his face. "What do you want?"

Jack held out the pie and she smiled down at him. "This is my nephew, Jack. Jack, this Mr. Clevenger."

"Pleased to meet ya."

The neighbor managed a grumble.

"Several of the apples from your tree out back fell into my yard. I also took a few from the branches that extended over the fence."

"Stealing my apples, are you?"

"I baked you a pie with them."

Jack held it out. "We're sharing."

"Humph." He looked closer. "You bake that, missy?"

"Yes sir, I did."

"Uh huh, well you any good at baking?"

"I think so."

"My wife Wanda was the best cook in the county."

"I'm sure she was."

The rich aroma filled the tiny porch. "You put cinnamon in there?"

"I did, with sugar and butter."

"Humph." He sniffed.

Jack had the pie high over his head. "You want it, Mr. Clevenger? Cause if you don't, I'll eat it."

"Now, don't go getting greedy, young fella."

The elderly man took the pie. "I'll try it. Don't expect much though."

Cora stifled the grin that threatened. She didn't want to anger the man. "I hope you enjoy it."

"Don't count your chickens."

Cora and Jack smiled victoriously as they turned to go. She knew Mr. Clevenger wouldn't be easy, but there was just something about the old man she adored.

"And dab nabbit don't go stealing any apples from my side of the fence."

"We won't," they said in unison.

With Jack tucked into bed, Cora warmed up a cup of coffee, donned her sweater and moved out to sit on the front porch. She had to fix those steps before someone broke their neck.

She dreaded the work week ahead. Bart grew bolder and more aggressive each day. No one had said anyway, but Cora felt she'd be the first one in Bart's office come Friday.

She took a sip of coffee and watched a car drive by. She noticed it was the sheriff's black and white. Didn't the guy ever sleep? He seemed to be everywhere. He stopped in front of her house and rolled down the window.

"Things okay, Miss Williams?"

She stood, gripping her cup. "Yes, I'm just going in." She turned and swiftly entered the house and flipped the lock. Leaning against the door, she willed her heart to slow down and stop getting all out of whack when the man came close to her.

She was beginning to wonder if she feared he'd arrest her and take Jack away, or was there perhaps another reason

.

CHAPTER SEVENTEEN

Next morning, Virgil went to the county courthouse, two doors down in the square. He walked up the steps and went into the judge's chamber. The honorable Francis Garner sat at his desk rolling a cigarette. He wore his customary black suit with a matching vest and a white shirt.

Judge Garner was born and raised in the house he still lived in. He was probably the tallest man in town at six feet, six inches. Skinny as a rail and tougher than any hardened criminal that ever marched into his court. At seventy, he still held the honor of being the best shot in the county.

"Mornin', Virgil." He waved him inside. "What you up to?" He struck a match and lit his smoke. "How was your weekend?"

"I've been keeping busy. You know how it goes."

"Sit down and take a load off."

"I gave Bart a pretty good dressing down about Adeline."

He took a long drag and blew out the smoke. "Heard she's back in Joplin."

"John put her on the bus."

"Good, let's hope she stays there because there's nothing here for a girl like her unless she's willing to go out to the edge of town and work for Mable as a whore, again."

He chuckled, he'd been there before. "You aren't supposed to know about that place."

"You'd be surprised at the stuff I know."

"No, I wouldn't."

"Anyway, I know this isn't about Bart and Adeline. What's on your mind?"

"I have a new person in town. A Miss Cora Williams. Rose Williams' niece. She has a nephew with her. It appears she was sent to prison for attempted murder."

Judge whistled. "Was it her fist time?"

"I don't know. I'd like to find out, but I don't want to go sticking my nose where it doesn't belong."

"Why are you so interested in her? She tickle your fancy?"

"No, but Mae said she was a doctor and a good surgeon. I just wondered how she ended up in the slammer for five years."

"Hum, I'll check around. Find out who the judge was and maybe learn something. I'll let you know."

"I'd appreciate it."

"Tell John I said hello. And tell Frank I hope he enjoys his new fire truck. I worked my fingers to the bone convincing council how important it was."

"I'm sure he's grateful."

Virgil walked out and went to his office. The day started out with the sun shining, but over to the west, clouds were building up. If his guess was right, there'd be rain later this afternoon.

John had just come back from checking out the local businesses on Main Street when the phone rang. John picked up the earpiece and put it to his ear. "Okay, I'll be right out there."

"What's happening?"

"Looks like old man Trenton is on the rampage again. He's threatening to shoot Lester's dog for killing his chickens."

"God, why can't people get along?"

"I'll go with you."

CHAPTER EIGHTEEN

Cora showed up at work and the ladies chatted about how their weekend had gone. Several customers came in to pick up and drop off laundry. Bart wasn't there and that made them all happy.

"Has he ever missed a day," she asked, hoping for a day of not having to be on her toes.

"Once in a while he's so hung over he can't make it in, but that don't happen too often."

Just then Bart walked in and grumbled to the women before going into his office and shutting the door. Ma Baker muttered under her breath and kept scrubbing.

Cora continued ironing and helping with the laundry. The day started out pretty, but dark clouds loomed in the distance. They'd be lucky if the sheets dried before the rain set in.

She helped a few customers and Bart came out to rant and complain about how lazy they all were, and that he should fire the whole damn lot of them. But he didn't. Before long he went to lunch and they sat down to eat.

"God, that man is in a fever pitch today."

They'd just finished eating when the bell over the door rang. Cora got up and went to the front of the store. Bart's wife and daughter stood waiting.

"I'm sorry, but Mr. Cooper has gone to lunch."

"He wasn't at Betty's Diner." His wife wrinkled her brow. "Wonder where he's eating."

Not willing to get into trouble, Cora wasn't about to tell on Bart. "I don't know."

They turned to leave. "We'll come by later."

"Mrs. Cooper," Cora said. "Did you find a dress for Alice?"

"No, nothing was good enough."

Twisting her fingers, and hoping she didn't step over the line, Cora said. "I don't know if it would interest you or not, but I have a dress designed by Christian Dior that I wore only one time. I'd consider selling it."

Mrs. Cooped backed away, suspicious. "Where did you get a dress like that?" Her thick brows rose almost to her hairline.

"My father bought it for me." She lied.

Alice's face lit up like the 4th of July. "Momma, I'd love a *designer* gown."

Nose lifted, Mrs. Cooper replied, sourly. "I don't know."

Alice grabbed her mother's arm so tightly she flinched. "Please, let's at least look at it. Christian Dior makes fancy dresses for all those movie stars in Hollywood."

"I'm not sure we should."

"The dress is a soft baby blue. It would look stunning on Alice."

"Momma, please." Alice tugged on her mother's hand then reached up to hug her. "It sounds so dreamy. Like something Elizabeth Taylor might wear." Releasing her mother, Alice folded hands under her chin and batted her eyelashes. "Pretty please."

Mrs. Cooper sighed. "When can we see it? And how do we know it will fit?"

"Can you drop by Friday in the late afternoon? Alice can try it on then." Cora pointed to Nell. "If the gown needs altering, she'd be more than happy to tailor it for you."

"Okay, we'll see you Friday."

Alice took her hand and squeezed. "Thank you, Cora. I'm so excited."

She watched them leave. She'd planned on keeping the dress until she ran out of money then sell it, but this might serve her purpose better. Bart deserved to be exposed for being a liar and a cheater.

"You're playing with dynamite, girl." Helen warned. "He'll fire you for sure."

"I'm expecting that, but at least his naive little wife will learn the kind of man she married."

Nell came over and took her by the hand. "But, you won't have a job."

"I know, but maybe this will help you ladies. You shouldn't have to lay with a boss to get paid."

"We all know it's wrong, but that's the way Bart does business."

"Maybe it's time that stops."

Nell leaned over and kissed her on the cheek. "We're going to hate losing you. You a fine lady."

Would they feel that way if they knew the truth? If they learned she'd nearly killed a man?

After Bart returned, no one told him his wife and daughter had come by the store. Drunk as a skunk, he stomped and shouted most of the afternoon.

Cora and Ma Baker had run out and taken down the laundry before the rain started. They barely made it back inside the store before the skies opened up.

They were busy folding the sheets when Sheriff Carter walked in. Cora went to the counter. "May I help you?" She thought he'd come to talk to Bart again.

"Come to pick up my laundry."

Struggling to remain calm, she forced herself to relax and smile. "I'll get that right away."

Taking his slip and rummaged through the bundles until she found his laundry, she set the brown paper wrapped bundle on the counter. Then she hung his three freshly ironed uniforms on a hook.

"Thank you."

Helen had already told her that the sheriff wasn't charged for laundry as that was a service the town provided for his dedication to duty.

Bart came out scowling and stood in the middle of the store, his fists jabbed against his waist, his beady eyes staring at the sheriff.

"Day, Bart."

"Sheriff."

The tension grew until finally Sheriff Carter took his things and left, the bell tinkling gently in the loud silence.

When the sheriff closed the door to his car, Bart approached Cora, his face red. "Don't be too friendly with the sheriff if you want to keep your job."

"I'm just giving friendly service to all our customers."

He slapped her on the rear and turned and stalked back to his office. All the girls turned away as her cheeks burned.

Avoiding the puddles, Cora ran to pick Jack up from school. He and Tommy ran ahead of her, but waited patiently at each street for her to give the okay to cross. After spending the day sitting at a desk, the boys had energy to burn.

Maggie stood outside waiting for her kids to return from school. "So, how'd it go at work today?"

"Well, Bart whacked me on the butt."

"Considering what he's capable of, be glad he didn't throw you on the floor and have his way with you."

"You're right."

Watching the kids running around, Maggie said, "God wasted all that energy on them."

"I know. What I wouldn't give to feel like running a race." She looked inside the open door. "I see Briggs is home."

"There wasn't any work today at the mine. Since the war ended there's barely enough to keep the few employees working."

"During the war lead and zinc were in heavy demand. Now, that's not the case."

Maggie slung the cup towel over her shoulder and sighed. "I wish he could find something else."

"Jobs are so hard to find." Cora noticed the worried lines on her friend's face. "It's difficult in most places."

"My brother just left for California. Gonna go pick fruit."

"I hope you don't have to move, Maggie. You're the only friend I have."

"I plan on staying right where I was born and raised." She watched Briggs limp across the porch. "I know his wound from the war hurts, but with the kids and the rent, he has to keep working."

"I understand."

"I guess if worse comes to worse we can live with my folks. I hate to do that because the kids drive my dad crazy. But, we all have to make sacrifices."

Just as Cora started to excuse herself to go start dinner, the sheriff drove by. Maggie waved. "Hey, Virgil."

"It seems every time I turn around he's there."

"He's not one to sit in his office and do nothing. He knows this county and the people in it like the back of his hand." Maggie pulled her sweater closer. "We're all just grateful he made it back from the war."

He'd told her he was in the Marines but she hadn't thought much of it. War had to be horrible. "I'm thankful for all the men who came back and I pray for those families who lost loved ones."

"Our Virgil came back a hero. Got awarded a bunch of medals. But he, like Briggs, never talks about the war. I think it's just too hard for them to remember all that killing."

"Was he the sheriff before he left for the war?"

"No, his daddy owned the filling station on Main Street and he always worked for him. Then the war started and after his older brother signed up, Virgil did too."

"His family live in town?"

"At the edge, out on D Highway. Only his folks are alive. Both brothers were taken by the war. His mom and dad never got over the loss. His dad sold the station and the county offered Virgil a job. He was always honest and cared about people."

"I'm surprised he's not married."

Maggie put her hands on her hips. "My, aren't we curious."

"Not really." She turned to hide a smile. "Just making conversation."

Jack ran up and he and Cora started home.

CHAPTER NINETEEN

The week had started off with a bang for Virgil and it had stayed that way. He left Betty's Diner and expected to go back to his room and call it a day when the fire engine alarm clanged down Main Street.

Every man in town ran toward the fire as flames licked the sky behind the old livery. Virgil ran to his car and hit the siren. Several cars followed behind him to the site of the fire. Frank pulled the engine closer and several men ran to Jacob and Doris Poole's house.

Flames shot out the windows in the front of the house and the roof. Three children huddled in the front yard next to a big maple tree. Jacob, wearing only his long johns, stood outside throwing a bucket of water on the blaze.

Frank pulled up the truck and ran with the hose to the fire hydrant. Virgil had already unscrewed the cap. They secured the hose and started spraying down the house. Several men continued to throw buckets of water on the flames.

Virgil looked at the crowd and saw Cora and Jack. She walked over to Poole's children and put her arms around them and led them to the street so they'd be out of harm's way.

Jacob and Doris's house was almost burned to the ground. It had been a dry summer and Jacob had fallen asleep with a cigarette in his hand. Luckily, he was the only one in the house. His wife was at her sister's with the kids and they came running when they saw the smoke.

Virgil pulled Jacob away from the fire to safety before he ended up burned to a crisp. Cora had gone for the first aid kit in the fire truck. Gently taking Jacob's hands, she put cream and bandages on his burns.

One of the men had been cut by a piece of metal and she took care of that. Virgil grabbed one ladder and the Frank was on the other. With axes, they chopped holes in the roof trying to clear away debris so there wouldn't be anything to burn.

Maggie and a few ladies brought coffee and sandwiches while Cora helped those injured. When Virgil came back down, she came up to him.

"What will happen to the family?"

"The church will help out and do what they can."

"But their home is gone."

"They'll probably move in with Doris's sister."

There was no doubt they'd be taken in because that's what people did in times of a disaster.

"You have a cut on your arm."

He looked down. Covered with soot and grime, he wondered how she managed to see anything.

She sat him down and washed the wound. "This isn't too bad. But keep it covered so it doesn't get infected. You see it turning red, go to the doctor."

"You're a doctor aren't you?"

She straightened and her eyes widened. "I was. I'm not any longer."

Jack hurried up, a sober expression on his face. "Sheriff, I never seen a fire before."

"Not something anyone wants to see."

"I'm sorry they don't have a house anymore."

Virgil patted him on the shoulder. "They're all alive. That's what matters, Jack."

After the excitement died down, Cora took her nephew's hand to go back home and get ready for bed. Virgil wished he had a place of his own. Instead, he stayed and cleaned up with

Frank. All the burned furniture that couldn't be salvaged had to be hauled away.

When they were finished, Frank slapped him on the shoulder. "Let's go to Rock Bottom and have a beer."

"I'm for that. I'll follow you back to the station."

The honky-tonk sat on the outskirts of Gibbs City where locals went to relax and shoot a game of pool. The beer was cold and the booze watered down, but Virgil didn't care.

"Nothing like a cold beer after a fire."

Taking a sip of beer, Virgil said, "What a dang fool for smoking in bed. There should be a law against that."

"Well, it cost his family everything they had. I know he has work, but it's going to take a long time to get back what they lost."

Virgil leaned his elbows on the rough counter. "Yeah, and they'll never be able to afford to buy another house. I feel bad for Doris and the kids, but they'll be okay."

"I saw that Cora Williams at the fire helping out. She's cute."

If Frank only knew. "She's a woman with a past."

"Why'd she lose her medical license?"

Virgil looked at his friend. "She went to prison for trying to kill a man."

Frank whistled. "That's powerful. And is that the reason she lost her medical license?"

Virgil turned his beer in the condensation ring on the table. "I don't know all the details, but I'm curious."

"You interested because she's pretty?"

"No, because it seems a little unfair. And, I can't imagine why the hospital here wouldn't hire her to do something. Judge told me he would check out a few things. I'll go from there."

"Well, good luck with the hospital. You know what a hard-ass that administrator Elbert Levy is. I don't think he likes a single person and no one likes him."

Virgil took another sip. "Yeah, he's a hard nut to crack."

"He have a family?"

Thinking back, Virgil said, "Lives in Cartertown with his mother. I don't think he's ever been married or had a family."

"He doesn't have a lot to do with the folks around here."

"Well, I might pay him a visit. See what's going on."

"The hospital is always looking for doctors, according to Mae. Surgeries are way behind and it's hard to even keep the nursing department fully staffed."

Virgil raked his fingers through his hair then cupped the bandage Cora had placed on his arm. "I don't know. My guess is that a felon can't be a doctor."

"Can you get those things overturned?" Frank finished his beer.

"I don't know enough about the law to say. But, look at how many times Doctor Leers been arrested for being too drunk to drive and fighting with his brother."

"You might ask the judge. But, if she's any good, the town needs her."

"That's what I'm thinking."

He wouldn't confess to Frank what else he was thinking.

CHAPTER TWENTY

Cora took the Dior gown from the hanger and carefully folded the fabric and reverently placed the dress in a paper sack. If it became too wrinkled, she'd press it before Mrs. Cooper and her daughter showed up.

An air of uncertainty filled the dry cleaners as all the women were tense and weary. Today Bart would assert his authority and make them have sex with him. Cora had awakened that morning, a knot of nerves in the pit of her stomach. Even now, she worried her coffee wouldn't stay down.

At work, she hung the dress neatly on a hanger and slipped it on a hook next to the full length mirror Nell used for alterations.

Helen ran her hand down the front of the fabric, her eyes touching every inch of the satiny blue creation. Hand to her chest, she breathed. "My, that is one beautiful dress."

Ma Baker stood back, admiring the gown. "Mighty fine."

"Where'd you get a dress like that, Cora?"

"I bought it."

Nell's eyes grew big. "You must've been rich."

Not wanting to sound arrogant, Cora smiled softly. "I had some money."

"Was your man rich?"

"I didn't have a man."

"How in the world did you make the money to buy something that expensive?"

Turning to face her co-workers, Cora filled her lungs. "I was once a surgeon and worked as a doctor in a hospital in St. Louis."

Helen folded her arms and cocked her head. "If you're a doctor, what are you doing here?"

"The State took my license. I can't practice anymore."

Ma Baker lowered her brows and looked her in the eyes. "What'd you do?"

"Something I shouldn't have."

A customer came in and the conversation ended. Cora didn't want to bare the whole ugly truth right now. There would be little understanding or sympathy from anyone once they knew what she'd done.

The day dragged slower than a late train, making Cora's nerves taut and had her jumping at every sound. As the afternoon rolled around, it surprised her when Bart didn't leave for lunch. Instead he strutted around the store smelling like a cologne factory and smiling like a sewer rat.

Acting giddy, he lightly tapped her on the nose. "You're going first today."

"First at what?" She knew exactly what he referred to.

"Don't tell me these bigmouths haven't told you what I expect before I hand over your paycheck. You gotta earn it."

"I thought we had by working two weeks."

"Well, today you give me a little something extra and you get to keep your job."

She'd learned Friday afternoons were the slowest time of the week. That gave them a chance to catch up on all their work so they stayed busy. But not busy enough to forget what awaited them.

About two thirty in the afternoon, Bart called out from his office. "Cora, get in here."

She stole a glance at the other women. None would meet her gaze, instead fear and resignation dimmed their features and gloom slowed their steps.

A moment's reprieve came when a customer walked in. Cora hurried to wait on the mayor's wife. Counting out the change, Cora noticed Bart looking out his glass window and he didn't appear happy. Deliberately, she took her time and started a conversation with the customer about the weather prolonging her departure.

Finally the lady left. "Get in here now," Bart ordered gruffly. The other three women jumped, lowered their heads and returned to busy work.

Just as Cora turned to walk toward Bart's office, she caught a glimpse of Mrs. Cooper and Alice getting out of a brand new DeSoto. Relief sent blood surging to her head and she staggered slightly. Before they entered, Cora reached up and grabbed the bell as she opened the door, waving the ladies inside.

"Follow me, please," Cora said, walking to Nell's work area. When they stopped, Alice's eyes teared and her mouth opened, but she couldn't speak.

In awe, Alice whispered, "I've never seen anything so beautiful."

"You can try it on in your father's office."

The young girl gripped her mother's arm. "Oh, momma, I love this gown. It just has to fit."

Bart couldn't see them, but he could see the counter and he probably noticed there weren't any customers.

"I ain't calling you again, Cora," her boss shouted. "I said get in here now."

Spinning around at the sound of Bart's commanding voice, Mrs. Cooper put her gloved hand to her lips, her eyes round in shock. "Dear, what's he so upset about?"

Cora put on her trusty poker face and shrugged. "I don't know. He simply said he wanted to give me my paycheck."

Mrs. Cooper squared her shoulders, and with her daughter hugging the prized dress, marched into the office. Cora followed.

Bart stood in the middle of his office with his pants down around his ankles and his penis sticking straight up. When he saw his wife, his eyes widened with utter disbelief. "What are you doing here?"

Alice screamed and spun around, her back to her father.

Mrs. Cooper wasn't so calm, either. "Bart Cooper, just what do you think you're doing?" She looked at Cora, who avoided her gaze. "Did you call Miss Williams in to take care of that?"

Bart's hands shook like leaves in a storm and he stammered his words. "This isn't what it looks like."

"It looks like my daddy is not going to be too pleased with you, Bart. Now pull up your damn pants and get home."

Tears and shocked filled their teenage daughter's eyes. "Momma, I'm so ashamed. Does daddy do naughty things with these women?"

Bart buckled his belt and went to Alice and put his arm around her shoulder. "Of course not. Your daddy," Bart's words stumbled and he licked his thick lips as sweat popped out of his pores and trickled down his forehead. "I would never do that. I love you and your darling mother."

Mrs. Cooper grabbed her daughter and put her behind her to shield the young girl from her father. "Then what are you doing with your pants down calling one of your workers into your office?"

"I was just adjusting my pants and they fell..."

"Stop lying."

Mrs. Cooper turned to Helen. "What's going on here?"

Helen refused to say a word, but Ma Baker spoke up. "If we want to get paid, we have to bend over his desk and let him put his whacker in us. If we don't, he'll fire us."

"My word." Mrs. Cooper's face reddened and she clutched her fist to her chest. "I've never heard of anything so disgusting." She glared at her husband. "You get home. I'll deal with you later." She looked at the women then picked up their checks on the corner of Bart's desk. "Here are your paychecks and I promise you that no one will lose their jobs."

Cora accepted the envelope. "Thank you, Mrs. Cooper."

"Helen, here is the key, you lock up this afternoon and open in the morning."

"I have a key, ma'am."

"Good, don't expect to see Mr. Cooper for a few days and when he does come back there will be no monkey business going on in his office." She put her arm around her daughter and turned to leave.

Cora stepped forward and asked, "Mrs. Cooper. What about the dress?"

She held it up to her daughter. "I'm sure it will fit, but if it needs adjustment, we'll come in Monday." She then opened the cash register. "I'm paying you double your asking price for the dress."

"Ester!" Bart screamed.

"Shut up. This dress is worth twice that much money."

When they left, Mrs. Cooper had Bart by the ear and was practically dragging him to the car.

The women smiled and hugged Cora. "None of us would've had the nerve to do that."

"Don't get too excited. You know he's going to come back and probably fire us. Me for sure."

Helen hugged her tightly. "We'll face that when the time comes."

She left to pick up Jack with a much lighter heart than when'd she'd dropped him off earlier that morning. She wasn't sure her plan would work or what the outcome would be, she just knew there was no way she'd let Bart Cooper force himself on her.

Before leaving for work that morning, she'd put a roast in to slowly cook in the oven. Stepping inside, the aroma made her stomach growl.

She'd put her paycheck in her purse. Tomorrow morning they'd take it to the bank along with the money she'd made selling her favorite evening gown. That would give her and Jack a nice nest egg should Bart Cooper decide to fire her when the air cleared.

Friday evening meant no school for Jack tomorrow and they'd have the weekend together. As she finished preparing dinner, he handed her a sheet of construction paper with a picture he'd colored. In red and blue crayons he'd drawn a little house with a tree and a broken porch. Standing in the yard were stick figures of her holding Jack's hand, smiling.

Cora bit back tears. Their family. They were a family, just him and her. She taped it proudly on the icebox door. That drawing became the most precious item she had ever owned.

CHAPTER TWENTY-ONE

Virgil was on his way out the door of his office when the phone rang. It was a man he knew in St Louis reporting that Ted Young had been found murdered.

The thought disturbed him that maybe their conversation had something to do with his death. Exactly what went on in the prison? Always punctual and dependable, Virgil knew that come tomorrow Cora would report in as usual. Last Saturday he'd been out on a call, but John said she came in and reported that she and Jack were settling in nicely.

He could wait and talk to her tomorrow, but an unsettling urge pushed him to drive over to Rose's old house and talk to Cora. Perhaps she could shed some light on Ted's murder. Something in his gut told him there was more here than met the eye.

The minute Cora opened the door the scent of home cooking smacked him in the nose. He removed his hat and nodded. The smell of food had his mouth watering so much he hoped his stomach growling didn't give him away.

"Miss Williams, I wonder if you might have a few minutes to answer a few questions?"

She paled, her hand clutching the door tightly. "Am I in trouble?"

114

He smiled and smoothed the brim of his hat. "No, ma'am, not at all. It's just that..."

"Hi, Sheriff," Jack called out, running toward the door. "Come in and have supper with us. Aunt Cora made roast and we got plenty."

"*Have*, Jack," she correctly patiently. "We *have* plenty."

Face scrunched, he looked at his aunt. "That's what I said. Can the sheriff eat with us?"

While nothing would make him happier, Virgil didn't want to go where he obviously wasn't wanted. "That's okay, I can come another time."

He turned to go, loneliness squeezing his chest.

"Sheriff Carter," she called. "You're welcome to share our dinner if you want."

Turning back to face her, he said, "You sure you don't mind?"

"Jack's right. We have plenty."

She opened the screen and pushed the door wide. Taking Jack's hand, she led him back to the kitchen. Virgil had been in the house on a few occasions but he didn't remember it being this clean, or welcoming. Rose kept a good house, but as she aged, so did the place.

Now the furniture shined, the floors were spotless and the kitchen a warm, welcoming sight. She offered him a seat and he pulled out a wooden chair.

Before sitting, he winked at Jack. "Thank you for the invite."

"You're welcome, Sheriff. This way if a robber breaks in you can shoot him with your gun."

Kids said the strangest things. "I doubt that will happen. We have a pretty nice town here."

Cora set a plate of roast, potatoes, carrots and sliced tomatoes in front of him. Rich, creamy gravy covered the meat and vegetables. He could hardly wait to dig in. If it tasted half as good as it smelled he'd have a meal to remember.

After passing Jack a plate, she sat down, putting Virgil between her and Jack, which placed him at the head of the table.

It almost seemed normal or fitting. Virgil couldn't rightly say. She poured iced tea and just as he picked up his fork, Jack bowed his head.

"Oh Lord, we thank you for this wonderful food, the warmth of this house and the love in our hearts. Amen."

"That was nice, Jack."

"I don't like doing it, but Aunt Cora keeps saying we're blessed, so it's only right to give thanks."

Virgil looked around the cozy environment. "She's right. You two are blessed."

Cora looked at him, a puzzled expression on her pretty face. Virgil's mother had never been a great cook and military chow wasn't fit for pigs, but this meal was delicious.

He cut a slice of the warm bread on the table and covered it with butter. He sunk his teeth into heaven. Cora Williams would make some lucky guy a wonderful wife.

He averted his gaze at the unusual path his thoughts were taking. But he couldn't help thinking of marriage when they were together.

"How's school, Jack?"

"It's good. I like my teacher, Miss Potter. She's nice." He filled his mouth then chewed slowly. "We have recess almost every day."

"Miss Potter is a nice lady. I see you and Tommy Cox playing together."

Jack beamed. "Tommy's my friend."

"He's a good boy. Has a nice family, too."

"Did you fight in the war?"

Cora cut in. "Jack that isn't polite."

How could he spoil this moment? "I did."

"Tommy said you got lots of medals."

"Some, but so did a lot of other men."

"Can I see your medals sometime?"

"I don't rightly know where they are." He knew exactly, but he rarely opened that box. "I'll let you know if I come across them."

Jack finished first and asked to be excused. When Cora mentioned dessert, he told her he'd have it before bedtime. Then out the back he went, slamming the door in his wake.

Virgil wiped his mouth with the checkered napkin Cora had laid beside his plate. "I think that boy's britches are on fire."

She grinned, her eyes riveted on Jack's exit. "He just wants to play a couple of hours with Tommy before they both get called in for bed."

She scraped a carrot off her plate and popped it in her mouth. "You look like you're enjoying the roast."

"This is the best food I've had in a long time. Where'd you learn to cook like this?"

She glanced around and lowered her voice. "The first job I had in prison was in the kitchen. I didn't know how to boil water, but Ellie Fry taught me how to stay alive and how to cook." She gazed into the distance. "I'll always be grateful for that."

His stomach full, Virgil stood and took his and Jack's plates to the sink. Pausing to scrape the dishes over the trash, he rinsed off the plates while she lit a fire under the coffeepot.

While the coffee perked, they cleaned the table and she took a pan of cobbler out of the oven. "Is that dessert?"

"Yes. The peaches are from a can, but I think it'll be okay." She scooped him up a bowl and poured them both a cup of coffee. "Do you take cream or sugar?"

"No, black's fine."

Virgil didn't think he had room for the cobbler, but one taste and he knew he wouldn't be leaving any leftovers. When he finished, he leaned back and rubbed his stomach.

"That was a wonderful meal, thank you, Cora. I certainly appreciate the invitation to join you tonight." He pointed at the extra cobbler. "Jack must have a sweet tooth."

"Oh, that's for my neighbor, Mr. Clevenger. There were some apples in the yard, so I made him a pie."

"If you can get along with that man, you're the only one in the county that can."

A childish smile lit up her face. "He's a little rough."

"He's down right ornery."

"I'm glad you joined us for dinner. When you were standing at the door, you looked like you needed a good meal. I don't like to turn anyone away hungry."

"You're kind."

"You said something earlier about a few questions."

Scooting back his chair so he could turn and face her, he asked, "Do you remember a guard, Ted Young?"

Her face turned to a blank page. "Yes, I do. He was one of the few decent men in that place."

"He was found murdered this morning. He'd been stabbed in the back."

Her hand covered her heart and fear widened her eyes. "That's horrible." She twisted her hands. "I've been in town all day and I..."

He held up a refraining palm. "I don't think you murdered Ted. I wanted to ask you if you might know of someone with a reason to want him dead."

She thought for a few minutes. "He treated all the women with decency and respect. None of them would've harmed him." She nibbled her bottom lip. "I can't speak for the other guards."

"What bothers me is they found his body in your old cell. I'm thinking maybe someone who worked in the prison might have wanted to shut him up."

She swallowed, her face white as a sheet. Even her once pink lips were colorless. "I don't know anything about that."

She lied through her pretty white teeth and she was suddenly scared to death.

"I thought you might have some information certain people wouldn't want to get out."

She jumped to her feet. "I can't tell you anything, Sheriff. I wish I could, but if I learned one thing in there it was to keep my mouth shut. I'm sorry Ted Young was killed. He was a good man, but I can't help you."

"I'd never let anything happen to you. No one can reach you here."

She chuckled. "You have no idea."

"Then tell me."

"No, I won't risk my life. I have Jack to think of. And I won't put yours in jeopardy, either. Leave it alone and let them handle it in St. Louis."

CHAPTER TWENTY-TWO

Over coffee the next morning Cora thought about the sheriff having dinner with them. He'd been much more polite than she'd expected, however she couldn't completely trust him. She knew men could turn on a dime. Friendly and helpful one minute, out to get you the next.

Pain stabbed her heart that Ted had been murdered. During a brief conversation, he'd told her he had a wife and two little girls. How devastated they must be. To lose someone you love at such a young age.

Ever since the day she'd walked out of prison, Cora had suspected Ted had something to do with her early release. She had no proof and couldn't even think of a reason, but nothing that day had made sense.

Avoiding Sheriff Carter's questions had her struggling between right and wrong. Those who murdered Ted deserved to pay, but if the warden or the guards suspected she might have said anything, she and Jack would be next.

Not a chance she was willing to take.

There were leftovers from dinner last night, so she wrapped a pie plate with a dish towel and headed to the neighbor's house. She knocked.

When he answered the door, the same ugly scowl covered his weathered face. "You're becoming a regular nuisance. Don't you have your own home? You have to keep coming over here to bother me?"

"We had roast last night and I fixed you a plate. Thought you might have it for dinner."

He leaned closer. "I might." He locked his gaze with hers. "It any good?"

She smiled. "We thought so."

"Well, I'll try it."

"Did you like the apple pie?"

He rubbed his grizzly whiskers. "Wasn't as good as Wanda's."

"I'm sorry. Did you have to throw it away?"

He stumbled back, a shocked expression covering his face. "I ain't gonna throw away good food. Are you looney or something?"

"Poor you, it must've been hard to force yourself to eat my awful cooking. I'll be sure not to bring you anything that inferior again."

"Now, don't go acting like a smarty pants there, missy." He walked into his house without inviting her in.

She waited outside.

He turned. "Well, come on in. Don't stand out there like you don't have a lick of sense."

Cora walked into the living room and at one glance she surmised that nothing had changed in this house since he'd lost Wanda.

Dust swirled in the air and covered most things in sight. The rug should be carried to the town dump and the kitchen looked like a tornado had crashed through the room. Poor Mr. Clevenger needed someone to care for him.

"Here's your pie pan. I didn't wash it."

"I'll take care of that."

He pulled out a large paper bag and turned to look at her. "You like pecans?"

"I love them."

He shoved the sack at her. "Here, then take these. Pecan is my favorite pie."

She accepted the offering. "I'll try my best to make a better one this time."

"Make sure you do."

"Thank you, Mr. Clevenger"

He shooed her away. "Now, get on outta here. I got stuff to do."

"I hope you enjoy the roast."

"We'll have to see about that."

The rest of Saturday Cora cleaned and did laundry. That afternoon on their way to Howard Martin's for groceries, she met several more of her neighbors and decided Jack needed his hair cut.

They'd talked about going to the barber, but she'd yet to convince Jack it wouldn't hurt. Still, he sat outside with his shoulders hunched and his face all scrunched up like the world was about to end. They were waiting for their turn outside on a small bench when Maggie came by with Tommy. He didn't look happy either.

Cora smiled. "Where are you off to?"

"Tommy complained of a toothache last night, so it's off to Joplin so he can see the dentist."

"I don't want to do that," Tommy muttered, holding his jaw.

"Then stop eating all that candy. Every time you get a penny, it goes right to buying candy."

Cora's sympathy went out to the young boy. "Oh dear, I wish you luck, Tommy."

"It's going to hurt a lot."

Jack, his feet swinging like crazy, showed concern. "Gee, Tommy, I hope you don't die."

Tommy pouted. "I probably will."

"Well, try not to because we're having a party at school next week and you won't want to miss that."

Tommy brightened. "That's right. I gotta be there."

Maggie let out a weary breath and tugged on Tommy's hand. "Let's get this over with." Her friend glanced at her with a frown. "Why on earth are you paying for a haircut? Bring him over to my house and I can give him a trim."

"I'm just doing it this once to get it all evened out. I have scissors and a pair of clippers. I hope to be able to keep it up myself." She patted Jack on the back. "Besides, every young man needs to experience a barbershop."

"You'll enjoy your day better than I will."

"Good luck," Cora said.

Before Maggie left, Virgil came out of the barbershop, his hair shorter than last night.

He smiled at Cora. "Afternoon, folks."

"Hi, Sheriff."

He looked down at Jack. "You waiting to get your ears lowered?"

Jack frowned. "Yes, sir." He pointed to Tommy. "He's going to the dentist and will probably die."

Virgil frowned. "There's a lot less pain getting a haircut than paying a visit to the dentist."

Tommy wailed, "I don't want to go!"

"And I don't want to get my hair cut."

"Looks like you're both outvoted. I can see not wanting to go to the dentist, but what's wrong with a haircut?"

Jack shrugged. "I just don't need it."

"Well, a young man ought to stay nice and groomed for the ladies."

Tommy made a face. "Ew, we don't want no girls. We're going to be patchlors."

"You mean *bachelors*," Cora corrected.

"Yeah, that's what we're going to do. We don't need no girls."

Virgil rubbed his cheek, his gaze shifting to her. "The day will come when that changes."

"No, it won't. Me and Jack are going to go fight a war. We're not messing with *girls*."

"Let's hope that wish never comes true."

Maggie left and Virgil waved goodbye to her and thanked Cora again for the delicious meal.

She thought about his questions. And again felt bad that the guard had been murdered. There was an excellent chance that one of the other guards stabbed him because they feared he might say something to the authorities. She knew to keep her mouth shut and the thought that they'd committed the crime in her old cell sent a message to her loud and clear.

Sunday arrived cold and rainy. The town of Gibbs City lay blanketed by dark clouds and rumbling thunder. She and Jack attended church, but returned home afterwards to stay inside. Jack quickly grew restless confined. His friend Tommy was in bed with a swollen jaw from having a tooth extracted and in no mood to play.

After reading a little, she and Jack sat at the kitchen table and played cards while a chicken roasted in the oven. Again, Jack's little feet were swinging back and forth.

A loud crack of thunder and a flash of lightning made them both jump. Then they looked at each other and laughed. They listened to the radio and Jack sat with his face pressed against the window, looking out.

"There goes the sheriff."

"That man must work every day."

She didn't know, but crime probably rarely took a holiday and she'd only seen Sheriff Carter in his office once.

By Monday, Cora and Jack both were ready to get out of the house. Joining the other women at work, they all waited nervously for Bart to show up. When she walked in, the first thing Cora noticed was that the door had been removed from the office.

When Bart arrived, his whole demeanor had changed.

He wasn't actually nice, but he didn't say a word about anything, nor did he call anyone into his office. Cora felt sure she'd be the first to go. Instead he was polite but very guarded.

CHAPTER TWENTY-THREE

Virgil's week was close to becoming a nightmare. Trouble had been brewing since he'd seen Cora and Jack outside the barbershop. He received a call from Mr. Keller complaining that Carl had broken out his window. And damn if old man Trenton wasn't still arguing with Lester about his dog.

Sunday he drove to St. Louis to talk to the lead investigator about Ted Young's murder. Unfortunately, he learned very little from the trip and that disturbed him because the truth was hidden and that was the same as lying.

As much as he could tell, no one accused Cora of any involvement, which eased his concern. However, the way everything happened might mean this was a warning for her to keep her mouth shut. Of course, she was doing a swell job of that. He wanted to talk to her again, but decided not to push too far or she'd close down on him. Virgil didn't want to put a bigger wedge between them.

He liked Cora too much to lose what ground he'd gained. Being in her home was wonderful and he felt so comfortable he wanted to be there every day. But that wasn't smart. He had to keep his distance so she wouldn't run away.

But while he was in St. Louis, he learned a lot about her family. For one thing, her sister had been killed. Accident, the death certificate said, but the ME he talked to didn't agree.

125

Everything about Cora's involvement was hush-hush and he wasn't allowed to see the records without probable cause or jurisdiction and he didn't have either.

He drove by Carl's house. His friend was outside sawing a two by four. "What've you been up to?"

"Trying to fix the back door."

"Well, old man Keller at the real estate office said you broke his window."

Carl wiped the sweat from his brow. "He's a liar."

"Says he saw you."

"I got mad and stormed out, but I didn't do anything wrong. Besides, I was right here all night."

Letting out a frustrated breath, Virgil shoved back his hat. "I said I'd talk to you and I have."

"Hey, why don't you believe me?"

"Because you get drunk and do crazy things."

Virgil drove back into town and saw Cora on her porch watching Jack play across the street.

He got out of his car and walked to the porch.

"Afternoon, Cora." Virgil cleared his throat. "Is it okay if I call you by your first name?"

She nodded then scooted over. "What brings you here?"

"I just got back from Carl's. He's a guy I grew up with and went into the service with." He propped his foot on the bottom step. "Mr. Keller said Carl broke out his window last night."

She sat up, her brow wrinkled. "Last night I heard glass breaking. Next thing I know, the two Miller boys went running by. I thought they might've done something."

"I'll go talk to them. I don't like Carl being accused of everything under the sun."

She shook her head. "It doesn't take much. I think your friend might be innocent in this instance. You know, nothing keeps a man out of trouble more than a job."

"I've tried to find him work but he drinks too much and isn't reliable."

"Find him something he loves."

Virgil considered that. "Carl used to be a mechanic in the Army and he was pretty good." Maybe Virgil could come up with something at the filling station. They were always looking for someone to work on cars.

Virgil left and went to dinner at Betty's. Sitting at the counter, Reverend Charles Fuller sat down beside him. "I heard Cora Williams is an ex-con. Spent time in prison."

Virgil turned and gave him his hardest stare. "Who told you that?"

"Word gets around in a small town. I don't think we need that kind of person living among decent folks."

"We can't just kick people out of town. She's not bothering anyone and she paid her debt to society."

"Still, I don't think it's best."

Nothing harder to deal with than a self-righteous preacher. "That's not something you get to decide." Virgil swallowed the last of his coffee and stood. "Besides, aren't you in the business of Christian charity?"

He went back to the station, leaned across the desk and glared at John. "Who'd you tell Cora was in prison?"

"I might have told a few people. I didn't figure it was no big secret, is it?"

"It isn't something that needs to be spread around either. The woman deserves a chance and she's not bothered a living soul."

The deputy held out his arms. "I didn't mean no harm."

"Yeah, you did or you'd have kept your mouth shut. I don't like having a deputy that spouts off stuff. Things that people don't need to know."

John got huffy, took his hat off the rack and left to go home. So angry he wanted to spit, Virgil didn't care how upset his deputy got. He seriously considered firing the big mouth.

John had no right to go blab everything all over the place. That would spread through the town like a wildfire. And how on earth could he stop the talk from harming her?

Annoyed, he went to Judge Garner's house. "Howdy, Virgil, come on in."

The judge lived alone after losing his wife last year to cancer. Dressed in loose trousers, an undershirt and barefooted, he didn't appear so commanding.

"I came to ask you a few legal questions."

He sat down and leaned back. "Shoot."

"Does a doctor automatically lose his license to practice medicine by committing a felony?"

"No, not necessarily. That's left up to the State Medical Board."

"So, they had to vote Cora Williams out."

"Well, they probably voted against her since she'd committed a crime. They might have thought it best if she no longer practiced medicine."

"Can that be overturned?"

Judge nodded. "Yes, it can. She'd have to present her case and try to change the minds of a bunch of sorry-assed men who don't think a woman belongs in a white coat."

"But, she could apply?"

"Again, yes. But, it's tough, Virgil. These holier-than-thou bastards have probably closed ranks around her. My guess is they never wanted her to graduate medical school. When she did, and became better at her job than some of them, they considered her a threat."

"That doesn't seem right."

Judge shook his head. "It isn't. But, that's the way of the world."

"I doubt she'll reapply."

"If enough people spoke up for her, and if she presented a clean case, they might reconsider. But it's doubtful."

Virgil left and drove to the Gibbs City Memorial Hospital. It was small in comparison to the larger hospitals in Joplin and St Louis, but it served the community well.

He took the stairs two at a time until he'd reached the second floor. At the far end of the long hall, Elbert Levy walked toward him with a briefcase in his hand. When the distance drew short, Virgil called out, "Mr. Levy, can I have a word with you?"

Elbert adjusted his glasses and stopped. "Certainly, what can I do for you?"

Moving to the side of the hall so as not to obstruct the traffic, Virgil leaned against the wall and crossed his ankles. "Do you know a Doctor Cora Williams?"

Elbert narrowed his beady eyes. "No, I do not know the woman."

"But you're aware she's lost her medical license?"

"Mr. Williams, her father, did the honor of paying me a visit last month to inform me that the State Medical Board had withdrawn her license."

"You didn't find that strange that a father would travel all the way from St. Louis to tell you that his daughter shouldn't get a job in your hospital?"

Elbert puffed out his chest. "He did it out of respect for this institution. My God, man, the woman shot a man. She could've killed him."

Virgil shrugged. "Could be the man deserved to be shot. Ever think of that?"

"No, I have not. And I'm outraged that you insinuate that I should. She's too reckless and dangerous to practice medicine."

He pushed Virgil aside and stomped down the hall. This just went from bad to worse.

CHAPTER TWENTY-FOUR

Later in the week, Cora was busy washing dishes in the kitchen when a knock caught her attention. She opened the door and a woman with auburn hair and green eyes, about her age, stood on the porch. In her hands was a dish covered with a red napkin.

"I baked you and your nephew some cookies."

Surprised and pleased, Cora held out her hand. "That's very kind of you. Please come in. My name is, Cora Williams."

"I've heard your name before and wanted to meet you. I'm Mae Price. My husband is the Fire Chief."

"Come in and I'll put on some coffee. I met your husband the night the Poole's lost their home."

"That's tragic. I visited Doris last week and they're staying with her sister for a couple of months until they get back on their feet."

Mae Price was tall and skinny with dark curly hair that complemented her eyes. She wore a print cotton dress with an apron covering the front.

"It's good they have a place to stay. I felt so bad for the children. I wanted to help, but Jack and I have so little."

"The church stepped up and gave them food and clothing."

"Good."

"You and I met in St. Louis, at General Hospital."

Her heart raced for fear Mae had heard about the trial. "I'm sorry I don't remember."

"I was a nurse. Now I work at the Memorial Hospital here in Gibbs City."

"Oh, that's good for you. Nurses are very hard to come by."

Mae picked up a cookie. "Virgil said you lost your medical license."

She didn't know how he'd come by that information, but she didn't like him discussing her past with strangers. "Yes, I'm afraid that's true."

"Ever thought of trying to get it back?"

She shook her head. "No, that would be useless. They'd never reconsider."

"Why not apply as a nurse. We have several openings."

"I don't know what the sheriff has told you, but with my past, I don't think the hospital would consider hiring me to sweep the floors."

"You don't know until you ask. Nurse Jackson is a fair woman. Go talk to her. She might surprise you."

Could she dare?

After saying goodbye to Mae, Cora's thoughts immediately went to the hospital. Maybe they wouldn't be so hostile. She should at least try. But then hearing she could no longer practice medicine had come as a stunning blow. Could she take that kind of rejection again?

A few days later Cora went to the hardware store to pick up a few things to fix her steps. She hadn't been there before, but the employees' coolness shocked her. They practically threw her purchases at her. When she asked if someone could drop the lumber off at her residence, they told her no. She found that strange since Maggie said they delivered.

As she and Jack struggled to get the boards home, Caroline waved as she exited the drug store and that lifted her spirits. The real shock came when she reported for work the following day. Bart stood waiting for her at the counter with his arms crossed and an ugly scowl covering his face.

When she tried to go behind the counter, he blocked her way. "What's wrong," she asked.

"I just learned you're nothing but a jailbird. You're a convicted felon that doesn't belong in society."

Heat traveled up her body and she cringed. "I've paid my debt."

"I don't care," he sneered. "You're fired and I don't want to see your face again." He turned to the other women. "And if none of you like it, then get out."

They stared, shock bulging their eyes. "There's no need to take your anger out on them. They've done nothing."

"Well, little Miss High and Mighty, my wife was completely floored that you had the nerve to apply for a job in my business." He turned to the other women. "Starting this coming payday, everything goes back the way it was."

Shocked and horrified that Bart would be so cruel, she bit back tears. The looks of surprise then disbelief showed on her co-worker's faces, and cut deeply across her heart. People she'd once thought were her friends.

She had no friends and never would. She left trying to keep the tears at bay until she got home, but there was no stopping them once she turned off Main Street. Everyone would know now. She had to find a way to tell Jack.

Jack.

The poor, little boy would have to live with the stigma of what she'd done. The shame of it all. But, she had no place to run and hide. She had to stay here or there wouldn't be a roof over their heads.

Even if she left, what would keep the next sheriff from advertising her past to the world? She'd been kind to Virgil. Hoped he'd be different, but that hadn't happened. He was just like the rest. A blowhard who liked to gossip like a woman.

She neared her house and just as she thought she was within the safe confines of home, Reverend Fuller came out of the restaurant and stopped her.

"It's come to my attention that you've had a run-in with the law and spent time in prison. I don't think our church is for you and Jack anymore."

She couldn't believe her ears. Surely a minister of the Lord wouldn't be so cruel. "You're actually throwing us out of a church."

"I'm only thinking of my flock."

"You do know churches are for sinners, not perfect people? But I'll be happy to stay away from a man who judges so quickly."

"You understand, I'm only doing what's right for my parishioners and Gibbs City. Maybe you should find another place to live."

Reeling in disbelief, she pressed her hand to her chest. "You're running me out of town, too?"

"Of course not. It's just for the sake of the boy you might want to consider relocating."

She turned and walked away, her hands balled so tightly her nails cut into her palms. So much for Christian kindness. That man was a beast and a horrible human being. She arrived home and closed the door behind her. Then she went to her bedroom, flung herself across the bed and cried until the tears dried up.

What did she think would happen? Did she think she'd get away without repercussions? That there would be no people to deal with when the time came and the truth was known?

She washed her face and put on a pot of coffee. How on earth was she going to get a job with the whole town knowing the truth about her past? Mostly she worried about Jack. What would he do if Tommy turned his back?

Looking at Maggie's house, Cora decided it was time she talked with Maggie. She deserved the truth.

After turning off the coffee, Cora walked across the street and knocked on Maggie's door. When she opened it with a wide grin, the cordial greeting slowly slid off her face.

"What are you doing home?"

"I lost my job."

"Well, I figured that would happen."

"I was fired because I was in prison before I came here. I was arrested, tried and found guilty of attempted murder."

Maggie looked at her with understanding gleaming in her eyes.

"I'd like to tell you the whole story if you have time to listen."

"Come in. You're my friend and one mistake doesn't change that."

"Oh, it wasn't a mistake. I'd do it again if it wasn't for Jack."

CHAPTER TWENTY-FIVE

Certain that there was a cover-up at the prison, Virgil worried Cora's life might be in danger, but he had no proof and no way to get any.

He took his laundry to the dry cleaners to see her, but Bart stood at the counter, a nasty smirk on his face.

"Miss Williams not working today?"

"She's not working here, period. I fired her."

"Why?"

"She's a criminal and I don't want my customers subjected that kind of person."

Virgil had to fight the urge to pull Bart over the counter and beat him like a rug. "Certainly not a man of your caliber, huh, Bart?"

"She's gone and as the sheriff of this town you had a responsibility to tell the community what crawled into our midst. My lovely wife shouldn't have had to learn about that woman from her bridge club."

Virgil picked up his clothes. "I think I'll take my laundry somewhere else."

Bart's eyes widened. "But, I have the contract from the town to do your laundry."

"I'll pay out of my own pocket before I'll ever let you make a penny of the town's money."

He left and threw his stuff in the back seat of his car. It really ticked him off that Bart was such a mealy mouth. He knew Cora would be home, probably worried about the next place to look for a job.

He cruised by her house but didn't want to stop right now. First, he planned to go to the office and have a talk with John. Parking in front of the station, Virgil stayed in the squad car until his temper cooled a little.

In the office, John was talking on the phone. When he saw Virgil, he hung up.

"Morning, Virgil."

"John, I'm really close to firing you. Your talking just cost Cora Williams her job. Now, she's a woman alone with a child and no way to support herself. Are you proud of yourself?"

"You have to know that eventually the word would get out. Maybe she told someone."

"No, she was too ashamed."

"I just said it in passing at the honky-tonk. I didn't mean her harm."

"But you were so eager to gossip, you didn't consider what would happen. I'm worried that no one will hire her. You know once people serve their time, they've paid their debt. We can't go around judging and I need to be able to trust my deputy."

He left to keep from knocking John's head off his shoulders.

On the way to Cora's, where he hoped he could set things straight, Maggie jumped out in front of his car and flagged him down.

She opened the passenger side and shut the door. "Let's go to church."

"What?"

"Get a move on. I want to go to the First Baptist Church of Gibbs City."

Virgil didn't know what to think, but he'd never seen good-natured Maggie this upset. They arrived at the church and before he could talk to her and find out what her intentions were, she was out of the car and running up the walk to the double doors.

That's when he saw the rolling pin in her hand.

He quickly jumped out of his squad car and ran after her.

She burst through the entrance and screamed, "Reverend Charles Fuller, get your skinny ass out here."

Charles inched from his office behind the pews. "What is it, Maggie?"

She pointed the weapon at him. "You tell Cora Williams she wasn't welcome in this church?"

"I simply said..."

"I know what you said, you hypocrite. You told her it was best for the town she leaves. Well, let me tell you what's best for this town."

Charles held up his hands. "Maggie, there is no need to scream."

"Yes, there is. I'm either going to scream my head off or beat you half to death."

"As the minister of this flock, I have the right to make decisions that affect this church and the people of this community. I don't want a convicted criminal among us."

"Oh, that's nice. But it's okay for the minister standing up there preaching about holiness and righteousness to be a cheater, a liar, and the father of a bastard child. Huh?"

Charlie's face turned red as the beets from Virgil's father's garden. "What are you talking about?"

"I know about JoAnn and I know about that little girl Mabel and Jerry Croker took in as an *adopted* child. That's the baby JoAnn delivered and she belongs to you."

"You can't..."

"What? Prove it? Yes, I can. My sister delivered that child."

Charles picked up a bible on the nearby bleacher and clutched it to his heart. Raising his voice to the heavens and his hand to God, he said, "I've asked the Lord to forgive my indiscretions."

"Now you need to ask him to forgive you for being an over-bearing shithead."

"Maggie Cox. You watch your language." Drawing himself up, he pointed a finger at her. "I stand on my ground."

"Good, cause I'm telling Edith. I'll blab it to the whole county. I'll see you run out of town on a rail. Then we'll see how forgiving your wife is." She shook the rolling pin. "Don't you think I won't."

Backed in a corner, Charlie's demeanor changed. "What can I do?"

"You can start by apologizing to Cora."

"Okay, I'll do it."

Virgil stepped up. "Get in the car. You're doing it now."

Charles threw down the bible and pointed to his office. "But, I'm working on my sermon for Sunday."

"I think you need to work on your soul today." He stepped aside. "Get in the car."

They drove to Cora's house. Maggie went across the street to her own place, the rolling pin still tightly clutched in her right hand. Virgil shoved the preacher up the broken stairs.

He knocked and she cracked the door slightly and peered out. "Yes?"

Charlie removed his hat. "Miss Williams, I've come to apologize. I was very rude to you today and I'm sorry I said such harsh words. You and your nephew are welcome in my church as long as you wish."

She opened the door wider. Her eyes touched on Charles then clashed with his. "Thank you, Revered Fuller."

Charles turned. "There, I've done it. Now take me back to the church."

Virgil shoved his hat back. "I'm not a taxi cab. Start walking."

"But..."

Virgil moved closer, wanting to slug the man in the nose. "I said start walking."

Virgil watched as Charles took a wrong step, stumbled and sprawled out on the concrete sidewalk. When Cora instinctively went to help him, Virgil held out his arm, barring her. "You gotta watch that first step, Reverend. It's a killer."

As Charles huffed off, Virgil tipped his hat and looked down at Cora. "May I come in?"

"Why, so you can learn more gossip to spread around town?"

"I never uttered a word about you. But John, my deputy, did and I'm thinking on suspending him for a week without pay."

She opened the door and he stepped inside. The aroma of fresh coffee filled the house. Virgil remembered he hadn't eaten breakfast yet.

"Coffee?"

"I'd like that."

She looked out the window. "I hope the town doesn't start talking about the two of us being alone."

"We're adults. But people will talk even when there's nothing to say."

"Bart fired me this morning."

"I'm not surprised. I stopped by to drop off my laundry and he gave me an earful."

"I'm so sorry if I got you in trouble."

"No need for that. Your business is your own. You don't owe the people of this county anything. You've been a good citizen and a good person. There are those who aren't."

She put his coffee in front of him then cut a slice of some kind of apple spice cake. "You sure do a lot of baking."

"I never knew how before I went to prison, but I really love to bake."

He enjoyed his late morning with Cora, but he had too much to do to sit idle. The murder of the prison guard hung heavily on his mind and he planned to stop by today and see if the judge had learned anything.

Also, this evening he planned to pay Nellie Dunn a visit. He'd wanted to get to the bottom of some of his suspicions about Bart, but had avoided approaching his citizens about something so delicate. Now, it didn't matter. The truth had to be revealed and it was his job to see that justice was done.

CHAPTER TWENTY-SIX

Later, a knock sounded at Cora's door and she was beginning to think there was a sign in her yard inviting people to stop by and visit. A colored man of average height and weight, around her age, stood on the other side of the screen door, smiling. He wore a nicely tailored suit and a sharp looking fedora. "Hello, Miss Williams. My name is Joseph Johnson. Most folks call me JJ."

"I'm pleased to meet you. Won't you come in?"

"No, I don't want to bother you. Your Aunt Rose spoke of you often and I wanted to introduce myself."

"You knew my aunt? Was she your teacher?"

"Yes, I knew her but she didn't teach the colored children. We have our own school on the east side of town. And a mighty fine teacher, if I may say so." He smiled. "She's my wife."

"That's nice, JJ." She liked the young man. "You sure you won't come in?"

"No, I'm a lawyer and due in court soon. Miss Rose and my father were friends. He's doing poorly now. He wanted me to make sure I came by and introduced myself and let you know we both welcome you to Gibbs City."

"Thank you. I'm sorry you lost your friend. My Aunt Rose was a wonderful person."

"You and I met when you came to visit one summer. I doubt you remember."

"I do remember you and your father. Didn't he build the shed in the back yard?"

"Yes, he did a lot of work around this house. He's pretty handy. He used to own a lumber store."

"Please come in and let's visit, JJ."

"I can't right now, but Saturday I'll be around to fix those stairs." He pointed behind him. "Someone might get hurt."

"I'll pay you for your work, but I must warn you, I lost my job this morning."

"I wouldn't think of charging you a dime, Miss Williams."

"Call me Cora."

"I'll see you on Saturday and don't worry about the cost. Consider it a favor to your Aunt Rose."

She knew there was a thriving community of colored people on the other side of Main Street. During a summer visit, Aunt Rose had taken her there to have dinner at JJ's father's house.

Some coloreds worked in town like Nellie, but most were safely on the other side of Main Street before the sun went down. Kind of an unspoken rule.

She heard a noise out back and looked out the door leading to the yard. Mr. Clevenger stood on the other side of his chain link fence, calling her name.

"What is it, Mr. Clevenger?"

"Here's your plate back." He handed it to her. "Whatcha doing home from work at this hour?" He narrowed his eyes. "You sick?"

"No," she lowered her head. "Mr. Cooper fired me today."

"What for?"

Why keep hiding things from people. If her neighbor wanted to shun her then she had no way to prevent that from happening. "I was in prison for shooting a man."

He rubbed his bearded chin. "Did you kill him?"

She shook her head.

"Well, you should've. If a man's worth shooting, he's worth killing."

"I'm a convicted felon."

"Hell, girl, I've been called a lot worse than that."

"Reverenced Fuller banned me from the church, but I think the sheriff made him change his mind."

"It was probably Maggie Cox. I saw her tearing out of her house with a rolling pin."

Cora smiled. "I'm not sure what happened, but he apologized then he fell down the front stairs."

"Good. Should've broke his damn fool neck. That would've served the knucklehead right."

"Mr. Johnson, JJ, came by today and offered to fix the stairs. He's coming Saturday."

"That's a fine young man and he's as good a carpenter as his daddy. They both spent a lot of time with Miss Rose."

"How was the cake?"

"You're not half bad as a cook. The roast was a little tough." He glanced down at her and she smiled. "The taters could've cooked a little longer. Next time leave out the carrots. That's rabbit food."

"Next time?"

"How are you ever going to make a good cook if you don't have somebody pointing out your shortcomings?"

Cora laughed and put her hand to her throat and acted hurt. "My shortcomings?"

"I'm only trying to help you and you just don't have the sense to recognize good intentions when you see 'em, now do you?"

She inwardly smiled. "I'll work on that, Mr. Clevenger."

"Make sure you do."

"The cake? How was the apple spice cake?"

He fisted his hand and pressed it to the middle of his chest. "Gave me heartburn. Too much nutmeg. Next time, cut the nutmeg in half and use cloves instead."

He turned and walked away, Cora laughed all the way across the yard.

CHAPTER TWENTY-SEVEN

Virgil waited in the back of the courtroom for the judge to finish the trial then he asked for permission to speak to him.

He sat down, balancing his hat on his bent knee. "I'm thinking of putting John on suspension for two weeks."

"Why's that?"

"He let several people in the town know about Cora Williams' past and it got her fired."

"He should keep his mouth shut about stuff like that."

"I have to say, I'm not too happy with him as a deputy. He talks too much, doesn't take the job as seriously as he should and he's too damn quick to judge."

"Those aren't good qualities in a lawman."

"No, and they lead to a lot of problems that I usually end up taking care of."

"Why don't you fire him?"

"I hate to fire anyone who needs a job."

"In the matter of keeping the peace, it's important a man meets a certain standard. Trust is as important as dedication"

"I think the suspension will help. If not, I'll file a request to fire him." Virgil resettled his hat.

"What have you learned about Miss Williams' medical license?" the judge asked.

"Not much. I spoke to Elbert Levy at the hospital and he told me that her father paid him a visit and basically instructed him not to hire his daughter."

"I checked with a bailiff I know in St. Louis. He says that, in his opinion, the whole thing was a set up. And the man she shot was Judge Martin's son."

"Did he preside over the trial?"

"No, but judges stick together. I'm sure that was all rigged against her."

"So, her father and a judge. Those are powerful enemies."

"My guess is the deck was stacked against her from the beginning."

"I've been checking into the guard that was murdered in the prison. I think him being discovered in Cora's old cell is a message for her to keep her mouth shut."

"That's probably good advice."

"Whatever it is, I don't want anyone coming into my jurisdiction and doing anything stupid, either. I want to send them my own message to stay away from Parker County."

"Best way to do that is to contact the Governor." He smiled. "Who's a good friend of mine, by the way."

After leaving the judge's chamber, Virgil grabbed a bite of dinner at Betty's and then went to the east side of Gibbs City. He pulled up in front of Nellie's yard.

She lived in a neat, well-cared-for house that her family had owned for years. On the well-lit porch, Virgil knocked and Nell's husband, Buford answered the door.

"Evening, Sheriff. Come on in. You had supper?"

"I just left Betty's. Is Nell home?"

"Yes, sir, she's in the kitchen doing dishes."

Buford opened the door. Virgil removed his hat and walked inside. Nell came out wiping her hands on a bright green cotton apron. "Hi, Sheriff, what brings you to this side of town?"

"I wanted to talk to you if I could, Nell."

"Sure, what's on your mind?"

"Can we step outside?"

Nell and her husband exchanged worried looks. "Is anything wrong," she asked.

"No, I just need a little information."

Nell removed her apron and stepped out on the porch. "What's wrong?"

"Bart fired Cora today."

"I know he did. He's been dying to put her in her place since the day she started."

"Did she deserve it?"

"Shoot. You must be kidding. That woman can iron better than anyone I know. And she ain't lazy, neither."

"I heard he found out about her past. But I have a hunch that's not the whole reason he let her go."

Nell studied the toes of her shoes. "That Bart Cooper is an evil man."

"I know that. What did Cora do?"

"First, I need to have your word you won't let this ever get to Buford. He's a good man and don't deserve to be troubled over what some crazy man did."

"You know you can trust me, Nell. I'd never do anything to harm you or your family."

"Since I worked there, every payday, we have to..." She averted her gaze. "We have to let old Bart have his way with us."

Virgil's gut burned like he'd swallowed a kerosene lamp. "Old Ma Baker, too?"

"Not her so much anymore, but Helen and me have to do it every payday." Her youngest child ran out into the yard. "I ain't even sure he ain't old man Cooper's. But I don't think on that."

"What happened with Cora?"

"Well, Mrs. Cooper wanted a fancy dress for that ugly daughter of hers. Miss Cora mentioned she had a designer gown she'd sell her. Mrs. Cooper jumped all over that. Miss Cora set it up for the time Bart usually starts calling us into his office one at a time."

"And he got caught by his wife?"

Nell laughed, bent over and slapped her thighs. "I wish you could've seen that man standing in the middle of his office with his pants around his ankles, his little wiener sticking straight up."

"Ester saw that?"

"Walked right in on him. He'd been yelling his head off for Miss Cora to come to his office. She went, but his wife and daughter were right there with her."

"What happened after that?"

"Well, old Bart was nice for a few days and we were all starting to think that everything was going to be okay. Then he came in and fired Miss Cora because his wife found out she was in jail."

"What's going to happen now?"

"We're right back to paydays being hell."

He put his hand on her shoulder. "I'd like for you and Helen to press charges, but I know that's a problem that would cause you both a lot of pain. But, I'm going to take care of this one way or another."

"Thank you, Sheriff. I hope Miss Cora is okay. I plan to stop by and see her tomorrow after work."

"I'm sure she'll appreciate that." Virgil put his hat on. "It's going to be hard for her to get another job no matter what Bart says or does."

"Well, then people are stupid." Nell pointed her finger at him. "She's too smart to be working at a dry cleaners. And she's the hardest worker I've ever seen."

"Let's hope things work out for her."

CHAPTER TWENTY-EIGHT

After being fired, Cora decided to take the rest of the week and get things done around the house. Besides, she wanted to hide away until the gossip died down. Hopefully, it would subside some soon.

She'd cleaned up the backyard. Under the over-growth she discovered that she had a couple of fruit trees of her own. Some flowers had been covered by the weeds and a partial chicken coop leaned against the back side of the little shed.

It would be much more economical to raise chickens than to buy eggs at the store. Looking around the yard, she decided she had plenty of space for a garden. Pulling weeds and cutting limbs was just what she needed to keep her mind busy.

Maggie dropped by and found her standing on a wooden ladder propped against a large tree. "You turned into a monkey?"

"Hi, Maggie. You have time for coffee?"

"I came over to invite you to lunch. It's nice having another woman to talk to. Being the only female in a house filled with guys makes me crazy sometimes"

Cora backed off the ladder and laughed at Maggie's remark. I'd love a houseful of kids." She straightened her blouse. "Lunch sounds wonderful."

On the ground, they walked across the street into Maggie's two-story house. It was a nice, neat house with room for a family with three rowdy boys.

Downstairs was a small living room with a fireplace, a formal dining room and a big, eat-in kitchen. That's where they settled to have lunch.

"Briggs working today?"

"Yes, hopefully they can keep him busy the rest of the day."

"What did he do before the war?"

"His family owned a furniture store in Joplin and Briggs did all the paperwork and took care of the accounts."

"Working in the mines is really a different kind of job."

"You can say that again. But, he has to make a living somehow and his family sold the furniture store a year before Briggs went into the service."

Pushing aside a worn catcher's mitt one of the boys left on the table, Maggie poured two glasses of tea and put a grilled cheese sandwich and a bowl of tomato soup in front of her. Cora's stomach growled. "This is quite a treat. I haven't eaten anything I didn't cook since the day I arrived."

"It's not much."

"To me it's a feast." She took a bite of her sandwich and smiled at Maggie. "Thank you for cheering me up."

"It's the least a friend can do."

"Thanks for putting the preacher on the straight and narrow path."

Maggie laughed. "He doesn't have any right to pass judgment on anyone. I just gently reminded him of that."

Cora opened her mouth in surprise. "Did you blackmail him?"

"No, I just jogged his memory, that's all."

They both laughed.

"So where are you going to look for a job next?"

"I don't know. Mae Price came to my house and asked me to consider being a nurse. I've thought about that, but I'm not sure."

"There's pretty slim pickings around here."

"You're telling me. I'm waiting for all the talk to cool down before I even try." She took a sip of tea. "Most businesses don't even want to take my money."

"That's too bad. I'd like to think we're better folks than that, but I guess we aren't."

"I think it's normal. People don't know me so it's easy to think the worst."

"But your aunt was a pillar of this community. She did a lot for these people and, while they might not know you, they knew her."

"I can't change their minds."

"Well, if it gets too bad don't take any guff. Tell Virgil."

"I'm not going to run to the sheriff every time something happens. Besides, I'm not sure he isn't the one who let the cat out of the bag."

"Oh, no, that's not true. Virgil would never do that. Now, his deputy, John is another story."

"He did mention his deputy, but I thought maybe he was just shoving the blame downhill."

"No, Virgil ain't like that."

"I hope he doesn't do anything to the deputy. After five years locked up in hell, I can survive anything."

"That's the spirit. Don't take anything from these people. We've all done things that should make us humble."

She thanked Maggie and left to return to her yard work. The front looked very nice after she cleaned out the flowerbed and nailed the boxes beneath the windows, even if they were empty. One of the shutters hung loose and she managed to fix that.

She'd tackle the stairs, but she wasn't that handy with a hammer. After mowing the grass, or really just weeds, she went to the back.

After hammering a few bent nails into the coop, she decided this weekend they'd buy chickens. The shed needed cleaning and a path cleared, but she could do that. She pulled everything aside and shoveled out the rat's nest and all the other junk.

Most of it she put in a wheelbarrow and hauled it to the dump. Everything else either needed oiled or repaired beyond her expertise. She'd check with JJ on Saturday. Maybe he could help her.

She went to the hardware store and bought a gallon of paint, a roller, and two brushes. The house looked horrible with the peeling paint and rotted wood.

"Whatcha got there," Mr. Clevenger said.

She held up the pail. "I'm going to paint the house."

"You don't have a ladder that tall. 'Sides, you'll probably kill yourself."

"I'm willing to take that chance. Maybe I can borrow a ladder to get the job done."

"You ought to stick to cooking. That's something you're good at."

"Really? According to you I can barely bake a decent pie."

"Well, you can cook probably better than you can paint. What are you going to do with one gallon of paint?"

"That's all I can carry."

"Carry? Have Henry deliver it."

"He says he won't. I think he found out about my past."

"He can't do that."

"He can and he did. You should've seen me and Jack carrying home the two by fours. We almost didn't make it."

"Don't go back there."

"But I have to. I'll need more paint. And I need a few other supplies." She put her finger to her lips. "Maybe I can use the wheelbarrow."

He shook his cane. "No you won't, by God. They'll deliver, or else."

"But he said..."

"Pay no never mind to what he said. What's the color paint you have there?"

She told him then went to get Jack at school. Miss Potter's coolness shocked Cora. Where she'd once been friendly

151

and kind, now she snapped and snarled like a mean dog. Jack went over to another little boy.

The kid's mother yanked her son away. "Don't let me catch you playing with *that* kid."

Cora bent down to Jack. "Wait right here, I'll be back." That said, she rushed ahead to the mother with the redheaded little boy Jack had tried to talk to.

Tapping her on the shoulder, Cora said, "Excuse, me. Might we have a word?"

The tall woman with a scarf tied around her hair scowled and stepped back. "Don't come near us. We don't want anything to do with your kind."

"My kind?"

"I heard you're nothing but a jailbird."

"You heard right, I did go to jail." Cora stepped closer, her chest inches from the other mother. "However, my nephew has never done a bad thing in his life."

No longer able to control herself, she put her finger in the woman's face. "You ever treat my child like that again and I'll snatch every strand of hair out of your head and hang it from the flagpole."

The woman's eyes widened and her face grew bright. "Well, I never..."

"I don't blame you, I'd never be so rude either. Leave my child alone. You have a problem with me, fine. But don't mess with Jack." Cora stepped closer. "You understand me?"

Gathering her child against her side, the woman broke into tears and ran away. For a moment, Cora felt awful, but then she looked over at Jack. He stood there all alone, the other kids moving around, but none engaging him. Cora caught Miss Potter's spiteful gaze.

She calmly walked up the stairs. "I can see the word is out."

Miss Potter was in her twenties but wore her hair and dressed like an old woman. "Gibbs City is a small community of fine people who know right from wrong. We don't take kindly to riffraff."

Miss Potter obviously didn't know the real Bart Cooper. "This is a nice town full of small-minded people who relish in another person's misfortune. You're young, Miss Potter. You have no idea what this world and circumstance can make you do." She turned to leave. "Be kind, Miss Potter. You could be next."

Jack ran up and took her hand. "Aunt Cora, who was that lady you were talking to? I like Bobby."

"Is Bobby her little boy?"

Jack nodded.

"I'm sure he likes you too." She smoothed down his hair. "What little boy wouldn't want a swell friend like you?"

She hoped and prayed that none of this would touch Jack and that the people of Gibbs City would come to accept them and forget her past.

After Jack left for school the next day, a man dressed in a suit wearing thick glasses knocked on her door.

She opened it reluctantly. The man squared his shoulders. "I'm Elbert Levy, the Administer of the Memorial Hospital here in Gibbs City." He pointed his finger at her. "I'm here to warn you that it will do you no good to come to the hospital and apply for a job doing anything. Mae Price talked to the head nurse about hiring you as a nurse, but I put a stop to that nonsense."

"You mind telling me why you're so hostile? I don't even know you."

"Your father, Mr. Williams, came to pay me a visit before you arrived." He raised his eyebrows as if to challenge her to speak. "We had a very informative talk."

"And while he was there did he make a major contribution to your hospital?"

Mr. Levy's face reddened and he stepped back. "I don't know how that could possibly matter."

"Believe me, it does. My father thinks buying people is the easiest way to get their cooperation." She pointed at his nose. "You see, he now owns you. If he's the kind of man who'd set out to destroy his own daughter, just imagine what he'd do to you if you displeased him?"

She slammed the door and flipped the lock. Sneaking a peek out the window she watched as Mr. Levy slowly made his way down her broken steps.

The pain of her father's deception cut her deep and she fought to keep tears in check. Not only was he hurting her, he wasn't doing his own grandson any favors either.

Mean and vicious. Those were the only words that described the man who'd raised her.

CHAPTER TWENTY-NINE

Virgil went to the hardware store to pick up a new claw hammer since his was missing. Loud voices carried from the back of the store. He went to investigate. Earl Clevenger was at the counter shouting at Henry and banging his cane on the counter.

He then pointed the stick at the owner's chest. "If you don't deliver Miss Cora's supplies like you do everyone else's in the county, I'm going to take this cane and make you a new neck tie. You hear?"

"I won't deliver to no convict's house."

"You will or I'll make sure not another customer comes in this store if I have to stand out there with my shotgun."

Virgil stepped closer. "What's going on here?"

Henry pointed at Earl. "He's threatening me."

Cora's neighbor turned to him. "He won't transport supplies to Miss Cora's house and that poor woman has been hauling stuff by hand. Her and that little boy of hers."

"Henry, you accommodate others."

"She's a criminal."

"Not anymore."

"I don't care. My customers don't like her."

"Your customers or you?"

"It don't' matter. I don't want her in here"

Virgil pushed back his hat. "Legally she could close you down for that."

Earl waved his cane. "Worse, the whole town can turn against you."

"They wouldn't dare. I'm the only hardware store in town. They'd have to drive all the way to Joplin to hurt my business. How they going to do that?"

Virgil leaned on the counter. "Well, it sounds like maybe this town needs another hardware store. One that treats all its customers the same."

"Don't go threatening me or my business. I'm the one man in town who can get you fired."

Virgil leaned closer, glaring. "You're one man who can try."

"You both listen to me. This is my business and I'll do as I damn well please. If the two of you don't like it, then go to hell. I don't like either of you anyway. Now get out of my store."

Earl shook his fist. "You'll be sorry you said that."

"Shut up, old man, before I come around the counter and throw you out the door."

Virgil pointed a finger at Henry. "I'm warning you to keep your hands to yourself or I'll arrest you. And I might add that would be my pleasure."

"Get out of here, the two of you. I don't want or need your business."

They left, but not before several other customers decided today they didn't need anything from Henry's Hardware.

Earl charged ahead. "He's not going to deliver her stuff. Best I just get it and they can haul it for me."

"I hate that old Henry is like that, but then he's always been a pain in my butt."

"He wouldn't even have a store if it wasn't for his pappy."

They both stood on the sidewalk outside Henry's Hardware. "I'll talk to Cora and ask her if Saturday I can take her to Joplin. We'll get what she needs from there."

Earl clamped his cane like a gun. "That's one way to do it, but how do we let the whole town know what a pisser Henry's being?"

"I think I'll find a way."

Virgil went to Cora's to find her on a ladder scraping paint off the house. He told her to get down and he'd do that. She refused. "This is my house and either I take care of it or I don't deserve it."

"I'm just offering to help like a good neighbor."

"You think I'm a woman and can't do manual work," she challenged, hanging on to the ladder with one hand.

"I know you can. It's just that you don't have to. I'll come by this Saturday and take you to Joplin to get the paint."

"I don't think that's a good idea. What will people say? Besides, didn't you tell the preacher you weren't a cab driver?"

"I have my own car."

"I don't know if that's wise. People will talk."

"Let them. They're going to anyway, no matter what we do."

"Still, I don't like it."

"Will you come down off that ladder before you fall?"

A stubborn frown tightened her features, but she safely made it to the ground. "There, satisfied?"

"I've been thinking about old Henry's business. No one in town likes the man. He's rude, mean and overpriced. I wondered if a new store wouldn't be better for the whole county."

"But who could manage that?"

"I'd like to think Carl could do it. Maybe Briggs, too."

"But do they have that kind of money?" Putting down her scraper, she brushed her hands together. "Maggie and her family are barely making it."

"I know, but if one big company would do all their shopping there, that might do the trick."

"Do you know of such a place?"

"I know a few, but taking them away from Henry and getting them to try something new could be a problem."

"And there's still the money."

"Yeah, it's hard for the town drunk to get a job, much less borrow money from the bank."

"That's true. Do you know the banker?"

"I know him, but that doesn't mean he'd let go of the money."

Shoving her hair from her face with her arm, she let out a deep breath. "I don't know what to do. How much would they need?"

"A couple of thousand dollars at least."

"That's a lot of money."

"Yeah, and there's no guarantee they'll make a go of it."

She stared at the ground. "I wish they at least had a chance."

"Well, we'll have to think of something."

"I'm sorry to be so much trouble. I want you to know if I had someplace else to go, I would. We simply don't have the money. Besides, Jack loves it here and I'm afraid he might not adjust so well to another place."

"You're here to stay." He jammed his hands on his hips and tightened his mouth. "Don't even think about leaving. I'm glad you're here." Virgil wondered where the hell that came from. He was getting so sappy he'd be wise to keep his mouth shut.

"Thank you."

"Be ready Saturday at eight. I'll pick you and Jack up and then we'll head for Joplin."

"I could take the bus."

He smiled. "I'll drive you."

"Sheriff, I..."

"Virgil." He shoved his hands in the back pocket of his pants. "You can call me Virgil."

As she ducked her head, he figured her face had turned red. "I'm okay with that, but you might change your mind." She lifted her head and their eyes met. "I was really rude today."

Virgil's heart sped up. "Why?"

"A lady was mean to Jack after school because she'd heard about my past. I sort of lost my temper." She rubbed her hands on her trousers. "I wasn't nice."

"Did you shoot her?"

Her head shot up and she narrowed her eyes. "That's not funny."

He shrugged, fighting back a grin. "Just asking."

After talking to Cora, Virgil went to check out the situation about Carl being accused of breaking the window at the real estate office. The two young boys confessed and Virgil wanted any anger Mr. Keller felt toward Carl forgotten. That didn't happen. The guy didn't want Carl back in his business any time soon.

Carl just needed a break. And so did Briggs. He was a good man with a good head on his shoulder. Why couldn't they get ahead? Also, Nell's husband, Buford, was one of the best liked people in town and the best mechanic. Because he worked for a cheat, Buford didn't make a lot of money and Virgil thought his boss took advantage of him being colored.

Virgil was returning from the real estate office when he saw several boys gathered behind the Goodman's old abandoned house. Jack stood bravely in front of three much taller boys. He had a rock in each hand. Little Ronnie stood right beside him, striking a prize fighter pose with his miniature fists held out in front of him, dancing around like a chicken.

Not liking the looks of things, Virgil decided he might need to listen should an adult need to intervene.

"You're not hurting him anymore," Jack threatened. "You got no right throwing rocks and hitting him with a stick. He's just a little dog."

"He's a mangy old mutt that ain't good for nothing," shouted the biggest kid.

Tommy joined his friends armed with a big tree branch. "You ain't gonna hurt that dog no more."

Virgil looked at the scraggily black and white, little terrier that'd obviously been abused and discarded. Evidently, Tommy, Ronnie and Jack were there to defend the poor pup.

"What you gonna do with him?"

Jack raised his arm. "I'm taking him home."

"Yeah, Jack's taking him home," Ronnie repeated. "He's his dog now."

The boys moved closer and Jack let go of a rock, hitting the bigger one in the shoulder. He quickly found another weapon and the three skinny boys looked ready to defend the dog to the death. The poor mutt had no idea how close he came to getting killed.

Virgil got out of the car when the bigger boys closed in on the three defenders.

Virgil stepped forward. "Howdy, boys. What are you all doing?"

Jack lowered his hand and the other boys found the toes of their shoes interesting. "Nothing."

"Well, then get along so Jack and his dog can go home. It's getting dark."

"That ain't his dog. He's just a mongrel."

"Whatever he is, he belongs to Jack. If anyone tries to harm that dog, I'm going to be talking to his parents."

The older boys took off. Jack knelt down next to the dog with his ears lowered and his tail between his hind legs, shaking like he was half frozen. This animal hadn't known much kindness.

"Let's get you boys home."

"You think Aunt Cora will let me keep him?"

"I'm not sure. She's pretty particular about keeping the house clean."

"I know, but he doesn't have nobody."

"Let's see how this irons out."

They took the dog to the back door of Jack's house. "Aunt Cora," he called out.

"Yes," she said coming around the corner. She stopped when she saw the dog. "What's this?"

"He's a dog."

"I see that, but what's he doing here?"

"Well, I saved him. Some boys were hitting him with a stick and throwing rocks at him. I figured he needed rescuing."

"So, you decided to help him out?"

"Yes, ma'am. But, if I leave him out there, they'll come back and they might kill him."

"Jack, we haven't discussed getting a dog. And he's covered in fleas." To prove her point, the dog sat down and lifted his hind leg to scratch behind his ear.

Virgil stepped up. "He probably just needs a good bath."

"So, you're in on this?"

He lowered his head. "I've always had a soft spot for an underdog. And what Jack says is true. No animal deserves to be treated poorly."

"Can we keep him, please?"

"Jack."

"I'll take care of him, I'll feed him and you won't even know he's here."

She pursed her lips then reached out and scratched the dog's head. Grateful for her kindness, the pooch licked her hand as if pleading his case.

She straightened. "Well, since this is both your idea, I'm sure the sheriff won't mind helping you give him a bath to get rid of the fleas." When Virgil went to complain, she raised a brow. He understood. He either helped Jack or the dog was out.

"Okay."

"Also, he stays on the back porch. There are a few blankets in the closet that will keep him warm. When it's really cold, he can come in, but his home is the back porch." She put her hands on her hips. "You both understand?"

They agreed.

Jack decided to name the mutt, Pal, because they were friends. Pal had a bath that no one enjoyed. He was fed a few scraps before finally settling on the back porch. The dog curled into a ball and fell asleep.

Cora put on a pot of coffee and before Virgil could say anything she slid a plate of scalloped potatoes with slices of ham in front of him. She'd obviously heated it in the oven while Jack and he got soaking wet washing Pal.

"I'm sorry about the dog, but I'm proud of Jack," Virgil said. "He stood up against bigger boys to help a defenseless dog. That takes courage."

"It could've gotten him hurt."

"People don't say much, but when you stand for what's right, they take notice. If you're not careful, you might be raising a lawman."

"Oh, dear."

Virgil looked at her and smiled. "Be careful, Cora."

She returned his smile. "I guess there are worse things a boy could turn to."

"I resent that."

"I'll bet you do."

CHAPTER THIRTY

Cora and Pal walked Jack to school the following day. Jack gave the dog strict instructions to stay close to the house and not get into trouble. The little terrier wagged his tail and licked Jack's face. Cora knew there would be no separating the two from now on.

Maggie came over as soon as Cora returned from the school. Briggs wasn't able to work that day because there wasn't enough to do. She nervously chewed her bottom lip.

"You might not be the only person looking for a job. If Briggs doesn't get something better soon, we're just not going to be able to make it."

"Virgil was talking about that last night."

"So, now it's *Virgil?*"

She lowered her eyes, slipped aside and popped Maggie with a towel. "Don't be sassy."

Maggie laughed. "Sorry, I just remember the first day I met you. He had you shaking in your boots. Now, it's Virgil."

Her face scorched.

"Yesterday, Mr. Clevenger confronted Henry at the hardware store for not making deliveries to my house. Virgil walked in and I guess the owner threw them both out. He was pretty mad. Said he wished he knew of a way to help Briggs, his friend Carl, and Nellie Dunn's husband, Buford, to open a decent hardware store."

"That takes a lot of money and that's in short supply around here."

"I know. But maybe we can hope for the best. In the meantime, Virgil is driving Jack and me to Joplin Saturday to buy enough paint to finish the house."

"It's a shame you can't pay someone to help you with that."

"Money's too tight, right now. I can't do much until I get another job."

"Well, the place looks pretty darn good just getting cleaned up. I'd forgotten how nice Rose used to keep her yard. She also had a goat that used to keep her grass chewed down when she got too old to use the push mower."

"I can barely get that thing to work for me."

"Well, JJ always did a lot for her. He treated her very kindly and those around here grew to respect him for being so generous with his time to a woman who'd served this area so well."

"He's coming over Saturday to fix the front steps. Maybe I should let him know I might not be here, but he's free to go inside and get a glass of water if he needs to."

Cora decided to make a list of the things she'd need from Joplin. Chickens were out of the question, but the local feed store carried chicks. Maybe they'd be better to do business with than Henry's Hardware.

She was double checking the coop, making sure nothing could get into the hen house when her neighbor called out from his yard.

"What's all that ruckus over there today? Can't you stay inside and bake something?"

Used to her neighbor's rough tone, Cora smiled. "There might be something in the oven right now."

"Well, go check on it and stop that god-awful banging." He pointed his cane at her. "I'm gonna take that hammer away from you. Why, I can't get a decent nap anymore."

"I'm sorry, but I have so much to do around this place. I'm trying to get the place into shape before winter comes."

"Well, you don't have to do it overnight. You have to learn to pace yourself."

"I can't. Soon I have to get out there and try to find another job."

"That ain't going to be easy."

"I know, but I don't have a choice in the matter."

"Get married. That's what most gals do. Find you a man to take care of you and Jack."

She shook her head. "I won't do that. I don't want a man."

"Why on earth not?"

"After what I went through in prison, I learned firsthand that men can be the most dangerous creatures in the world. Especially to a woman."

"Well, there's where you're wrong, missy. I was married to Wanda forty-two years and I treated her like gold. Never even raised my voice, much less my hand."

She smiled. "You're one of the few, Mr. Clevenger."

"Lots of good folks around here. What about Virgil Wade? The sheriff sure is a spiffy looking guy."

"No." She shook her finger at him. "And don't go spreading rumors."

He narrowed his eyes. "I'll spread anything I want to, little lady, and you can't stop me. But, you ought to know by now I don't mean you or Jack no harm."

Ashamed, she lowered her head. "I'm sorry. It's just if the people around here thought something was going on between Virgil and me they'd think even less of me. Then I'd be a loose woman."

"I better not hear anyone say that. They'll get my cane shoved right up their..." He stopped and cleared his throat. "Let's just say it won't be pretty."

"I'm waiting for all the talk to settle down, then I'll be out looking for a job."

"I heard the county clerk was thinking of retiring."

"I don't think I'd be eligible for a job like that." She lowered her voice. "Remember I have a record."

He scratched his head. "I'm not sure what that all entails, but I might look into it."

"Don't waste your time. There are plenty of good folks who qualify for that job. I don't want to cut anyone out."

"You need a job, don't you?"

She nodded.

"Well, let me see what I can find out." He turned to leave. "Go check what's in the oven. I smell something burning."

Cora laughed and went about her business. She knew exactly how much more time those two pecan pies had to bake.

When the pies finished baking, Cora turned off the oven, changed clothes and set out for the east side of Joplin. After asking for a few directions, she soon found Joseph Johnson's office, very neatly situated between Doctor Nathan Wesley's office and an insurance company.

She knocked on JJ's door and a pretty young woman answered and invited her in. "I only need a moment of his time."

If she was surprised a white woman would ask a colored lawyer to represent her, she didn't show it.

JJ came out smiling. "I'm pleased to see you, Miss Cora."

"I only wanted to let you know that I might not be home when you come to fix the porch steps Saturday. But don't hesitate to use the house if you need it."

"Thank you, but that little job shouldn't take me more than an hour."

"It would take me a week."

They laughed as they sat on the couch in his office.

"Are you still looking for a job?"

"Yes, but there is something you need to know about me. I..."

"I know about you being in prison. Rose told me. That can make it hard for you to get a job, but not impossible. I believe in looking on the better side of things. I'm confident you'll find something."

She stood and smiled. She really liked JJ. "Thank you for that. My spirits needed a lift today."

"Come and see me anytime you want."

"The same goes for you."

She left to go get Jack from school and realized how much she'd enjoyed her chat with JJ. For some reason she felt close to him, maybe because he and Rose had been such good friends.

CHAPTER THIRTY-ONE

Virgil decided talking to Bart would do no good, but his father-in-law was another matter and Arthur Bridges held the purse strings. So, Virgil knocked on his door.

When Arthur answered, he seemed glad to see Virgil. Arthur Bridges was well into his eighties, but he was the healthiest man Virgil knew. He used to be a marathon runner in his youth and to this day, he had the body of a runner. Tall, lean, muscular, and still handsome at his age.

Wearing a Cardigan sweater, Arthur said, "Welcome, come in and have a drink."

"I'll settle for a cup of coffee."

Arthur sent the maid off to do his bidding. The Bridges were the most respected couple in Gibbs City. They lived in the biggest house in town and drove the nicest car. He'd made a fortune in the mines, land and several businesses he owned in town.

The real heartbreak happened two years ago when Arthur's wife died of pneumonia. Virgil thought Arthur would die with her. They were devoted to each other and Ester was their only child. She'd been raised by two parents who thought she could do no wrong.

Virgil settled in a comfortable chair with his coffee. He'd never taken to hard liquor and figured he was too old to start now. Besides, he'd seen what booze could do to a lot of people.

With a glass of whiskey, Arthur asked, "I don't see you much, Virgil. How are you?"

"I'm fine."

"How's life treating you?"

"Oh, I can't complain."

"What brings you out here this time of night?"

"You know, Arthur, I respect you and I'd never come to you if it wasn't serious."

"I'm aware of that. You're a good man. I've known you all your life."

Virgil leaned forward rubbing his hands together. "I'm doing this because I want to protect you and your daughter's reputation."

Arthur took a sip of his liquor. "Well, now I'm curious. Get on with it."

"It appears Bart has been demanding sexual favors from his female employee at the dry cleaners and that's against the law. None have come forward yet, but if they did there would be quite a scandal."

"How do you know this?"

"I've suspected it for some time. When Cora Williams went to work there I had a gut feeling he'd try to take advantage of her because she has a past."

"Is that the woman who sold Ester that lovely gown?"

"Yes."

"And did Bart make a pass at her?"

"She foiled his scheme by arranging for Ester to come for a fitting about the time Bart called her into the office."

Arthur gritted his teeth, narrowed his eyes and tightened his lips. "That good for nothing bum."

"I spoke to two of his employee and they've told me what's been going on. If one of them decides to testify I'm putting him behind bars and God only knows what that will do to your family's reputation."

Virgil knew exactly which card to play with Bridges. His standing in the community meant everything to him and he'd be hard pressed to let an insult slide.

Arthur's gnarled hands gripped the arms of his chair so tightly they appeared like paper with ink drawn lines. "I'll speak to Bart."

"You might as well know, your daughter caught him in the act and she's decided to let it go."

"Ester?" His eyes grew to the size of pie pans. "Ester!" he screamed.

Shortly Ester ran into the room, her hand clutching her chest. "My God, Daddy. What on earth is wrong?"

"What's this Sheriff Carter is saying about Bart?"

She turned aside, her cheeks pink, her eyes averted. Immediately the tears started flowing. "I went along with it because he said he'd tell my bridge club that he'd had sex with everyone who ever worked for him and destroy us." She wrung her hands. "What kind of woman do you think I am that I can't keep my husband satisfied? I'd be the laughing stock of town."

"Why didn't you come to me?"

"Daddy, I was so afraid and ashamed that I'd married such a man. I didn't know what to do." Ester seized Arthur's arm. "He promised he'd never do anything again." More tears. "Poor Alice saw the whole thing. I'm afraid she'll never stop crying."

"Okay, Virgil, meet me at the dry cleaners tomorrow morning."

"What time."

"Opening, eight."

"I'll see you there."

He left, not feeling one bit of pity for Bart. He was a lecherous old man who needed to be locked up for good. Virgil would run him out of town if he got the chance.

He decided to stop by Cora's and tell her what was going on. She poured him a cup of coffee and offered him a piece of pecan pie. Cutting into the delicacy, he opened his mouth and stepped into paradise. Cora made the best pie in the world.

She sat across from him. "I'm sorry about Bart but he deserves to be punished."

"He's a bully. Always has been and now he's even bullying his wife and daughter."

"I hate to see the women lose their jobs. They really need them."

"Let's wait and see what happens."

"I visited JJ today. I wanted to let him know I wouldn't be home Saturday."

"He's a good person."

She glanced down at the floor. "So, we're still on?"

"Oh yeah. Why don't we make a day of it?"

Her whole body looked tense. "I don't know."

"Come on, lighten up a little."

"I don't trust men."

"You know you're safe with me."

She chewed her bottom lip making it redder and riper than before. "I know that, but still."

"I don't want you being afraid."

"And I don't want to be hurt."

He left and went to the office. John had gone for the day. Since the deputy had been sincerely sorry for talking about Cora, Virgil decided not to suspend him, but gave him a stern warning.

He prepared for bed then went to Frank's to take a bath. His little room only included a commode and a sink. Several times a week he went next door for a bath.

Virgil thought about renting his own place. He needed a home now. How long could he stay in these cramped quarters before going crazy? Maybe he could build himself a little house on the property he owned on the outskirts of town. Living in a closet no longer suited him and it made him downright miserable.

Next morning, Virgil had an early breakfast at Betty's Diner and then went to the dry cleaners. Helen, Ma Baker and Nell were there, but Bart had failed to show up yet. He was about to open the door when Arthur Bridges' car pulled up and his driver opened the door. "Morning, Virgil."

"Arthur."

The elderly gentleman walked into the shop and the women stopped what they were doing and waited anxiously for Arthur to speak. Virgil thought they might be expecting to be fired.

"Ladies," Arthur began. "It's come to my attention there has been a great unfairness going on in my business. I don't like and won't tolerate any woman being mistreated."

The employees shuffled their feet nervously. No one looked at Arthur directly. Instead, they glanced at him to get a feel for what might be about to happen.

Ma Baker stepped up. "We're sorry if we caused any trouble Mr. Bridges. We never meant to."

"Miss Pearl, you've done nothing wrong and I intend to make things right." He pointed at Helen. "Haven't you been here the longest?"

She swallowed. "Yes, sir."

Bridges looked around. "Why in the world are you still washing clothes by hand and hanging them outside to dry. You need new equipment."

Nell lifted her head. "Mr. Cooper he don't want to spend the money."

"It's not his money. Everything belongs to me." Putting down his cane, Arthur took off his coat and hat and went into Bart's office. "Isn't there a catalog around here somewhere?"

The smile on Virgil's face grew wider by the minute. And today was *payday*.

"There used to be one over there on the shelf." Nell pointed. "I'm not sure what's in it."

Arthur pulled it down and all four of them had their heads together and fingers pointing. Oohs and aahs filled the room. Virgil leaned against the wall, crossed his ankles and grinned. He'd give anything if Cora could be here to see this.

"Okay," Arthur said. "Today, Helen, you order everything you ladies need."

Just then, the bell rang and Bart bounced through the door, an angry scowl on his face. He didn't see Arthur in his office. "What are you doing behind the counter, Virgil? Helen, you women get your asses back to work. Just what the hell do you think you're doing? I'll fire the lot of you."

Arthur stepped out and met Bart's glare boldly. "About time you showed up."

"Arthur, how nice of you to pay us a visit." Bart's face underwent a drastic change. He hiked up his pants and waved a beefy had toward the counter. "As you can see, we're doing just fine."

"Not according to what the sheriff says."

Bart swung around and glared at him. "He's a liar and that little whore of his is nothing but trouble. Both of them are."

"Bart, you're fired. You no longer manage the dry cleaners." Arthur held out his hand. "Give me your key."

"Wait a minute. Now, just hold on, Arthur. I've worked here for years. I've fiddled with this little shit job when you could've easily promoted me to a management job in the foundry or made me the manager over all your business affairs. Instead, I worked here like a common laborer."

"You were lucky to have this job. You've never had a business head and now I find you're treating the ladies under your employment like slaves."

"They're all liars."

"No, they aren't. But you are. Helen is now the manager with a raise in pay. All the women get a raise. You're not to enter this place of business at any time." Arthur grabbed his cane. "And I'll be taking a close look at your books, too."

"But where am I going to work."

"I don't know and I don't care."

"Think about Ester and Alice. Do you want them to do without?"

"They've both moved back in with me. You, on the other hand, not only have to find a job, you need a place to live."

Bart's father-in-law turned to leave the building. "You'll see him off the property won't you, Sheriff?"

Virgil tipped his hat. "It'll be my pleasure."

"If he comes back, Helen, call the sheriff so he can be arrested."

Helen and the other two ladies practically danced. "I will sir. But, might I ask one more thing?"

"Yes?"

"Can Miss Cora have her job back? She did the best work of anyone who ever held her position before and the customers really liked her."

"Then I suggest you put her back to work immediately."

Virgil saw Bart to the curb and warned him not to come back or there'd be hell to pay. "Nothing would make me happier than to lock up you up and throw away the key. You're worthless and now, without your daddy-in-law, you don't have much going for you."

"I know you're behind this. It's all because of that Williams bitch."

Virgil grabbed him by the collar and pulled him close to his face. "If you even think about harming her, going near her, or even mentioning her name with anything but respect, I'll find you and you'll be sorry you were ever born." Virgil shoved him away. "And if you utter a word about what went on here, I'll turn Helen's husband, Nell's husband, and Ma Baker's old son loose on you and I'll walk away."

Bart stumbled. "You can threaten all you want, but unless I break the law, you better leave me alone."

Virgil stomped his foot. "Don't push your luck. Now git."

Bart took off running down Main Street and Virgil grinned. It always felt good when the bad got what they had coming. He drove to the office to inform John and to warn him not to let Bart around the dry cleaner and to keep him away from Cora.

After he explained what happened, John was shocked. "I can't believe that man put those women through that. Bart better be glad Nell's husband don't know nothing about that. He'd break the man in two."

"I want this kept quiet. We don't need any more trouble."

"I agree. But now I like Bart less than I did before and I'm hoping he breaks the law so we can lock him up."

"Well, I'd be happy if he'd just go away."

"You gonna go tell Cora she's got a job on Monday?"

"No, I think that's Helen's place and it's best if it comes from her. The women at the dry cleaners really like her."

"She's a nice lady. I feel bad I ever said anything about her past."

"That's behind us. Let's just move forward." Virgil leaned down and stared at John. "It's real important that none of this gets out. Understand?"

John nodded solemnly. "Yes sir."

CHAPTER THIRTY-TWO

Saturday came quickly and Cora rose early to enjoy a leisurely bath before rousing Jack from bed. The weather had turned cold and Jack burrowed further into his pillow muttering a protest. A suspicious lump under the blanket wiggled then moved toward Jack's head.

Out popped Pal, wagging his tail.

In the kitchen, Cora made coffee and then whipped up a surprise for Jack. After a few minutes she returned to his bedroom. "I'm fixing chocolate chip pancakes today."

She didn't get to the kitchen before he came running past her. "What's a chocolate chip pancake?"

"It's a surprise, but I've heard they're wonderful."

He stood on his tiptoes to look inside the skillet. "It smells good."

A knock sounded at the door and Jack darted through the living room, Pal right behind him. The whole back porch idea hadn't gone over well with the two inseparable friends.

Jack flung the door open and Virgil's tall frame filled the opening. He wore a nice chambray shirt, jeans, and boots. He'd used a little Brylcreem on his hair and the aroma of bay rum tickled her nose. She smiled, flattered he'd spent extra time to look nice for her.

"We're having chocolate chip pancakes for breakfast. Want some?"

Kneeling to pet Pal, he smiled up at her. "That sounds wonderful, but I'd welcome a cup of that coffee."

"Jack's having 'special' pancakes, but I'll gladly fix you a stack of regular hotcakes."

He took two cups from the cupboard and filled them. "That's more like it."

They all sat at the table eating breakfast when Jack ran to get dressed. "I'll be ready to go in just a second."

"You wash your face and brush your teeth, young man."

"Yes, ma'am."

"He's full of energy."

"It isn't every day he gets to go to the big city of Joplin."

"Oh, I can imagine that." She wanted out of town as well. Gibbs City was a nice place, but right now, she felt the whole county suffocated her.

"Maybe while we're there he can catch a movie and we can do a little sightseeing."

"I don't know. I've never left him alone. What if something went wrong?"

"Listen, Saturday mornings all the young boys and girls are at the nickel movie for the matinee. It's 'Flash Gordon' and cowboys, and the 'Perils of Pauline'. Things kids like to see."

"I imagine that would be a lot more fun than going to a hardware store."

"You bet it will."

Before long they were in Virgil's Ford Coupe heading out of town with Jack in the backseat. Pal promised to stay on the porch and keep out of trouble.

The surrounding landscape took her breath away. The leaves were golden, red, and vibrant orange. Grass had turned to a sleepy brown and the sun shone bright. It was a perfect day and Cora was glad she wore one of her better dresses.

"So did Helen come by?"

Happiness made her want to laugh out loud. "Oh, I forgot to tell you. I have my old job back. Helen said Bart's father-in-law fired him and she's now the manager. Isn't that wonderful?"

"Best news I've heard in quite a while."

"I can't help but wonder how Mr. Bridges found out about Bart."

"Maybe Ester said something."

She put her finger to her lips and stared at him, hoping he'd crack. "Could be a certain sheriff I know went looking for the truth."

He smiled at her and Cora realized how handsome he was. His blue eyes were true and honest, his hair neatly combed and he looked spick-and-span. The hands gripping the steering wheel were sure and strong, his posture still held a bit of military training.

When she thought of the playboys she'd once dated, a laugh escaped her lips.

"What's so funny?"

"Nothing."

"Tell me?"

"Have you ever been in love, Virgil?"

"I have," Jack said brightly. "I love Sally Mann. She's the prettiest girl in the whole school."

"Wow, good for you, buddy," Virgil said. "But I thought you and Tommy didn't have time for the ladies?"

"We didn't, but Sally was selling kisses for a nickel."

Cora almost fell out of her seat. "Jack!"

"I didn't have a nickel, but I had two pennies and Tommy had two pennies. So, I thought that should be enough for each of us to get to kiss her cheek."

Virgil, hung his arm out the window, a big grin made his eyes sparkle. "Did it work?"

Jack shook his head. "No, she wanted a nickel."

"So what'd you do?"

"We had Ronnie promise he wouldn't steal her lunch anymore, if she took the four pennies and gave us both a kiss."

Virgil looked at Cora and laughed. "Did she go for that?"

Jack beamed. "Yep. Me and Tommy both got a kiss."

"Has Ronnie held up his end of the bargain?"

"Oh, he wasn't the one stealing her lunch, it was Butch Morgan. We told him if he took her lunch again, we'd give him a black eye."

"My Lord, Jack. You're too young to be in love. And no more buying kisses from Sally Mann and threatening to give black eyes. You have a lot of growing up to do first."

"I think you can love anyone at any age."

Virgil grinned and shifted the stick shift on the floor as they started up an incline. "Boy makes a lot of sense to me."

"This conversation should wait for a later time."

They arrived on Main Street in Joplin. The streets were full of people walking and shopping. Cars lined the street and a bus roared by on to its next stop. Big stores displayed all kinds of clothing, furniture, and wares.

A huge car dealership took up a whole corner.

They dropped Jack at the movie and told him to stay inside until they picked him up. Virgil made sure he had money for popcorn and a soda, and he checked with the ticket agent to see what time they needed to be back.

She tapped him on the shoulder. "You've avoided the question long enough."

"No, I've never been in love, and other than a few stolen kisses in high school, and other stolen things later in life, I can't say much about the fairer gender."

"I'd thought by your age, you'd have a family."

"How old are you?"

"Thirty-two."

"Do you have a husband?"

"No. Of course not."

"You're a year younger than I am. So why haven't you been married? I know a looker like you must've been fighting off the beaus."

"Not as many as you think. When you're a doctor, men tend to be a little intimidated, insecure and afraid of intelligent women."

"Hum, I must be really secure. I think the fact that you're a really smart woman is kind of sexy..."

Her eyes widened and her mouth made a perfect O. "What?"

He ducked his head and cleared his throat. "My apologies. I think it's nice that you're so smart. And I think you should fight to get your license back."

"Virgil, I'm not sure I want to go back to being a doctor."

He turned to her, surprised. "Really? But you worked so hard to get that degree."

"I did. And after I received it, I worked even harder. Long, grueling hours of surgery that left me completely exhausted. I have Jack now. Who would care for him while I'm putting in twelve to fourteen hours a day at the hospital? And don't forget, I'm just beginning to get used to freedom again."

"I see your point." They walked toward the hardware store. Inside, the smell of paint and grease filled the building. "But what about marriage?"

"I never considered getting married. I had a wonderful, successful career and all the finer things in life."

He pulled her aside, her back to the wall. "So then what happened, Cora?"

She shoved him aside. "I don't want to talk about it."

"You'll have to someday."

"Maybe, but not today."

Virgil insisted on buying the paint and he agreed to paint the house for her. She told him no, but he wanted to so badly, she couldn't keep saying no. According to Maggie, he didn't have much of a family life, so maybe he wanted to do it to keep busy. She knew how that felt, and at times she got lonely. After five years in prison she'd hoped for a new beginning with her parents.

How foolish.

She bought a few new things for the house now that she had a job, and even picked up a few dresses for work, a couple of pairs of jeans for Jack, and new couch covers. She added curtain material and new linoleum to replace the worn one in her kitchen.

Soon, she and Jack would have a home they could really be proud of.

On the way to pick up Jack, they parked in the parking lot and Virgil leaned closer. "The day is going to come when I'll know all your secrets, Cora."

She smiled. "Never."

Riding home in the car after shopping, her thoughts turned to tomorrow. They'd fix up their home, Jack loved his school, and she had Maggie and Mr. Clevenger.

Looking over at Virgil's handsome face, she tried imagining waking up to him every morning. The image wasn't clear, but it was close. Could she ever really love a man? Be happy to see his smiling face and able to stand his touch?

BOOK TWO

After grabbing a bite to eat, they drove back to Gibbs City to unload the trunk. When they pulled to the curb, Cora noticed her door stood open. Thinking JJ might be in the house, she didn't get concerned until she saw the new steps.

"Virgil, what's going on?"

"You and Jack get back to the car and stay there."

"Pal," Jack called. "Pal where are you?"

Cora had a feeling this wasn't going to end well.

BOOKS BY GERI FOSTER

THE FALCON SECURITIES SERIES

OUT OF THE DARK
WWW.AMAZON.COM/DP/B00CB8GY9K

OUT OF THE SHADOWS
WWW.AMAZON.COM/DP/B00CB4QY8U

OUT OF THE NIGHT
WWW.AMAZON.COM/DP/BOOF1F7Q9M

OUT OF THE PAST
WWW.AMAZON.COM/DP/BOOJSVTRVU

ACCIDENTAL PLEASURES SERIES

WRONG ROOM
WWW.AMAZON.COM/DP/B00GM9PU94
WRONG BRIDE
WWW.AMAZON.COM/DP/B00NOZMNSU
WRONG PLAN
WWW.AMAZON.COM/DP/B00MO2RFR8
WRONG HOLLY
WWW.AMAZON.COM/DP/B00OBS03M2
WRONG GUY
WWW.AMAZON.COM/DP/B00KK94F6G

ABOUT THE AUTHOR

As long as she can remember, Geri Foster has been a lover of reading and the written words. In the seventh grade she wore out two library cards and had read every book in her age area of the library. After raising a family and saying good-bye to the corporate world, she tried her hand at writing.

Action, intrigue, danger and sultry romance drew her like a magnet. That's why she has no choice but to write action-romance suspense. While she reads every genre under the sun, she's always been drawn to guns, bombs and fighting men. Secrecy and suspense move her to write edgy stories about daring and honorable heroes who manage against all odds to end up with their one true love.

You can contact Geri Foster at geri.foster@att.net